Samson &

The Siren

The Oliver Anderson Trilogy, Book Three

A Biblical Epic

by

Joshua David Jones

Samson and the Siren
The Oliver Anderson Trilogy, Book Three
© Joshua David Jones 2021
First Edition
ISBN 9798516783296

Cover illustration by Anthony DePietro of Depietrodraws.com. Cover designed by Stephen Melniszyn of Stephen Melniszyn Designs.

'Out of the strong, something sweet.'

To the faithful

1

SHE SCURRIED DOWN the hill at full speed, almost slipping in the dirt and gravel. If she could make a clean jump across the river at the bottom of this hill, she might put enough distance between herself and the cavalry.

She lifted her head and focused on the other side of the river. It wasn't vast, but the leap would require everything within her to make. She heard the sound of the horses neighing as they sought to navigate the steep landscape and the soldiers yelling commands to keep them steady.

If she got across, she'd be home. True, the soldiers would probably cross the water and pursue her even there. But, still, once she reached the other side, she'd be half a mile to the nearest town.

She measured her breathing, paced her strides, and looked at the opposite bank. *Five. Four. Three.*

And fall.

She'd been so focused on the opposite bank that she hadn't seen the jutting rock before her. She rolled forward to the bank of the river, tearing her bare legs and arms on the rugged terrain. Her body screamed with pain. She attempted to stand up but collapsed as soon as she tried. She'd twisted her ankle. It would no longer hold her weight. She glanced helplessly at the other side, hoping beyond hope that she might see Canaanite soldiers riding to rescue her. But it was absurd. There was no coming. Instead, she heard only horses and shouting in the tongue of Philistia behind her.

Even now, the fierce young woman wouldn't give up. She searched around for rocks, grabbed a few fist-sized ones, and spun around on her knees. She aimed at the closest soldier and hurled it, only to have the rock bounce off his breastplate. The six soldiers dismounted and tried to restrain her while she clawed and snapped at every Philistine hand.

A moment later, a black horse arrived. The young woman looked up and saw the one seated on it. A chill shot through her, and her head began to tremble. The rider on the black horse dismounted and approached her while unsheathing his sword. 'Well done! That was an impressive run you gave us. What was your name? Oh, it doesn't matter—you won't be needing it much longer.'

Samson & the Siren

She buried her fear and mustered up all the courage within her as she yelled at the demon. 'Go to hell, Philistine!'

The decorated officer laughed. 'Maybe someday, sweetheart, but not today. Do you care to tell me how long you've been spying on our garrisons near Ashkelon?'

'Long enough.'

'Hm, I thought so,' the general said as he stroked his black goatee. 'How many of the soldiers did you sleep with? You must be good at what you do.'

'Good enough to have given my people the information they need to take back the land that's ours,' she said with burning defiance.

'Between the land the Hebrews took on one side and the land we've taken on the other, you don't have much left—not much that's impressive, anyway,' said the general.

'We'll get it back, dog!'

'Dog? Charming. How about you let me know what the Canaanite leaders pay you? I'll triple it. I can do that—I'm a general,' he said and laughed. 'I hate to see talent thrown away like this. Work for me, and you'll find me most generous.'

She spat at his feet.

The general looked over at solder standing to his side. 'Do you see how she replied to my kind offer?'

'Yes, sir.'

The Oliver Anderson Trilogy

'Should I put up with insults from Canaanite dogs?'

'No, sir.'

The general spun around and brought the sharp point of his sword down on the woman's thigh, piercing to the bone. She screamed at the searing pain while the soldiers kept their grip on her arms. The general tossed his sword to the side and knelt on the ground in front of her. He grabbed her hair, pulled it back, and stared into her terror-filled eyes. He leaned forward and smelled her neck, taking in her scent. 'Canaanite sweat mixed with a Philistine perfume—the latest from the shops in Gath, if I'm not mistaken.'

Then the general pulled out a small dagger from his side. 'Hold her firm,' he instructed calmly. And, holding her head back to keep her gaze, he wiggled the dagger's tip slowly into her chest. He felt her heart pumping through his blade as he pierced into her life-giving organ. His dopamine levels soared, and his smile stretched from ear to ear in an erotic frenzy.

Her body spasmed for half a minute. The general watched intently as her eyes widened and then faded into a deathly glaze. After he felt the pumping cease, he stayed on his knees for several moments, embracing her. He didn't get to kill someone, especially a beautiful woman, like this every day, and he wanted to savour the moment.

Then Achish, the General of National Safety over Philistia,

stood and mounted his black stead. He looked over at one of the soldiers and said, 'When we get back, gather all the soldiers from the garrison. I need to give them a fresh warning about Canaanite whores—you can never be too safe.'

'Yes, sir,' the soldiers replied dutifully. And off they rode to the city.

The Oliver Anderson Trilogy

2

INVERNESS, SCOTLAND
21ST Century A.D.

'HELLO, I'M HERE to see my grandpa,' Oliver said soberly.

'What's his name, love?' the nurse replied, without looking up from her computer.

'Mr William Anderson.'

The nurse looked up. 'Oh, really?' she asked and paused. 'You're related to the Anderson fella, huh?'

'Y-yes,' Oliver said. 'What bay would he be in?'

'He's not in a bay.'

'Oh?'

'Yes. There were some difficulties, and we had to move your grandfather to a private room.'

Elise put her hand on Oliver's shoulder. 'D-difficulties?' he asked as a bead of sweat trickled down his back. 'Can I still see him?'

'Yes, he can have visitors. He's in room 52,' the nurse said, extending her left arm and pointing. 'Go to the end of this hall and take a left. OK?'

A nod was all Oliver could manage in response. Elise slipped her hand into Oliver's as they made their way down the hall. 'Did you hear that? It sounds bad, doesn't it?' he muttered, hoping Elise would contradict him.

'We'll see for ourselves,' she said.

'The nurse said "difficulties". That sounds bad, doesn't it?'

Elise squeezed his hand. 'You told me your grandfather was a man of faith. He'd want us to be brave.'

'Yes. Still, my only memories of him are as a bold Scotsman. I don't know if I can see him laid out on a hospital bed, filled with tubes, and near death's door.'

'You'll be able to handle it, Oliver.'

'Elise?'

'Yeah?'

'I know you've got those emails to respond to and all,

7

but I don't suppose you'd come in with me and—'

'Of course, I'm coming in with you,' Elise replied and gave him a loving pat. 'I didn't come all this way with you to sit in the waiting room with my laptop. I'll go in to see him—and do anything else you need.'

'Thank you,' was all Oliver could muster in reply.

As they approached his room, the door opened, and a nurse came out. She shut the door behind her, leaned back against it, and sighed at the ceiling. 'God, help us,' she muttered, turned and walked down the hall in the opposite direction.

Oliver froze. 'That's room 52 she came out of, isn't it?'

Elise took a couple of steps closer to the door. 'It looks like it.'

'I can't do this. If my grandfather's condition has shaken that nurse, what do you think it'll do to me?'

Elise wrapped her arms around him and pressed her body against his. 'Oliver,' she whispered, 'whatever you face today, know that I'm with you.'

He looked into her eyes. 'I can't thank you enough for coming to Scotland with me. Especially with everything that's happening in London.'

Samson & the Siren

'Nevermind about my problems back at the college. We need to go in and see your grandpa now. Even if he never regains consciousness, you'll regret it if you don't see him one last time. What if this is your last chance?'

Oliver sighed. 'You're right.' He approached the room and wrapped his hand around the doorknob. He turned to Elise. 'Ok, I'm ready. Let's do this,' he said and pushed the door open.

They stepped into the room and what they saw sent a jolt through both of them. Grandpa William was sitting straight up in bed with a book in his hands and his glasses on. 'Oliver!' he cried in his deep brogue. 'So good to see ye! Any chance ye can spring me out of this hellhole?'

The Oliver Anderson Trilogy

3

'OLIVER STRUGGLED TO get the words off his tongue 'G-grandpa? You're not, um, you're not—'

'I ain't what?'

'I mean, you're conscious.'

'Of course, I am. Do ye think I'd lie around unconscious in a place like this? These nurses are liable to stick somethin' unnatural up your bum hole when you're not lookin'.'

Oliver's face lit up. 'It's good to see you as... yourself.'

'Aye, well, who'd ye expect? St. Peter?'

Elise stood, wide-eyed, at the man before her. 'Oliver? Is this your—'

'Yes, of course.' Oliver said. 'Grandpa, this is Elise. Elise, this is my grandpa, William.' Elise stepped forward and extended her hand. William took it tenderly.

'So nice to finally meet ye. Though what a beautiful girl such as yerself is doin' with my grandson, only Heaven knows.'

'Cheers, grandpa,' Oliver said with a shake of his head. He then walked up to the bed and extended his hand.

'Watchya doin' with that hand? Give me a hug, laddie.'

'Can I?'

'Course ye can! I ain't broke.'

Oliver leaned down and embraced his grandfather. He was surprised at how much strength the older man still had in him as he squeezed him back. 'Wow, grandpa, you look great.'

'How else should I look? I'm an Anderson—great is what we do.'

'But, you know, your heart attack and all.'

'Maybe a wee little heart attack would take out an Englishman and have him all sorry lookin'. But ye need to remember that we're Scotsmen—and these wee sicknesses won't be controllin' us.'

'But the nurses,' Elise said, 'they told us something was wrong.'

'Yeah, grandpa. Why did they give you a private room? And that nurse that just left—she seemed upset.'

'And upset she should be! That banshee tried to poison me.'

Elise gave William a bewildered look. 'Huh? Poison?'

The Oliver Anderson Trilogy

Oliver was suspicious. 'What exactly do you mean by "poison" you?'

'Look at that tray over there,' William instructed. Oliver and Elise turned to see a food tray on a wheeled cart pushed against the wall. 'Ye see what's on it?'

'A fruit cup, strawberry yoghurt, a piece of white toast with spread, some green plant I don't know the name of, and a cup of coffee,' Elise said. 'You say there was poison in this?'

'It's why everyone in this place is so sick. It's the rubbish they give 'em to eat. I asked for bacon, eggs, sausages, and regular black coffee—but they say I'm not allowed it. So instead, they bring me this stuff. And, for lunch and dinner, they give me a plate of rabbit food.'

'They're called "salads", grandpa. It's what people eat nowadays—especially in hospitals.'

'No wonder they're all sick.'

'At least they gave you coffee.'

'I should be so lucky. Those nurses gave me decaf. Real coffee ain't good for ye if ye've had a heart attack, they say. Same with that off-white goop they gave me with the bread—if that stuff came from a cow's tit, then I'm a horse's arse.'

Elise choked on a laugh.

'Look, I know you don't care for this food, grandpa. But I still don't understand how you got a room to yourself.'

'Oh, that,' William said and looked away.

Oliver looked at his grandpa suspiciously. 'What did you do, grandpa?'

'Well, perhaps I might've expressed some of my views to the other patients a bit enthusiastically. And perhaps, just maybe, they took on some of my perspectives.'

'Your "perspectives"?' Wait, did you turn the other patients against the staff, grandpa?'

'I think "against" is a rather strong word for it. I merely told the other patients that I thought the hospital should feed us human food instead.'

'All nice and calm, huh? OK, then what happened?'

'As a group, we politely made our requests known to the stormtroopers.'

'They're called "nurses" and "doctors", grandpa.'

'Sadly, the authorities didna listen to our thoroughly reasonable requests,' William continued. 'So, some among us thought we needed to take our movement to the next level.'

'Your "movement"?' Oliver rubbed his forehead. 'What'd you do then?'

'We started a hunger strike.'

Elise gasped. 'A hunger strike? The in a hospital?'

'Just on our floor. It seems the patients agreed that the hospital should give us food that comes from nature and not a factory.'

'So, when they gave you a private room,' Oliver said, putting the pieces of the puzzle together, 'they were essentially putting you in isolation so that you wouldn't cause any more trouble.'

'Lad, I'm telling you, it ain't right. It's like a prison. Have ye come to break me out?'

Elise burst out with laughter. Oliver had told her about his grandpa's personality, but experiencing it for herself was more than she was prepared for.

'Well, grandpa, you're sure making a great first impression on my girlfriend. As for breaking you out, sorry, our visit has a far more modest aim.'

'Whatchya here for if not to help me regain my liberty?'

'We thought you'd nearly died.'

'Ah, I see. Ye came to say goodbye before I go up yonder, eh?'

'Something like that.'

'Well, don't just stand there, have a seat.' Oliver and Elise pulled up two chairs from against the wall and brought them close to William. 'Well, if yer not here to break me out, did ye bring anythin' to help an old man?'

'Grandpa, we didn't think you'd be conscious.'

Elise turned to Oliver, 'Should I buy some flowers?' she asked—which only caused both Anderson men to chuckle. 'W-what'd I say wrong?'

'You didn't say anything wrong, babe,' Oliver said, taking her hand, 'It's just that, well, grandpa doesn't care for flowers.'

'It's a lovely thought,' William said, 'But I'm a bit allergic. Now, if yer boyfriend here was worth his salt, he'd've brought me some beef jerky and my whisky flask.'

Oliver snorted a laugh. 'You want me to sneak whisky into a hospital?'

'Well, if ye ain't breakin' me out, I could at least have somethin' to help me cope.'

'Sorry, grandpa. I don't even have a flask of milk on me.'

'Well, I suppose that's OK for now,' William said with a wink. 'I've got somethin' stronger than whisky to help.'

Elise shot him a curious look. 'Oh?'

'What are you talking about, grandpa?'

'Shut the door first,' William instructed. Oliver got up and closed the door. Once he had, William turned and pulled something out from under his pillow and held it up for Elise and Oliver to see.

'A Bible?' Elise asked.

Oliver grinned. 'I'm glad you've got the Good Book, but I don't think it's against hospital rules to have one.'

15

'Ain't it? Give it time. If they haven't forbidden this book yet, it's only because they don't know what's in it.'

Elise smiled, and Oliver raised an eyebrow. 'Sure you're not exaggerating a bit, grandpa?'

'Lad, this book has led to the downfall of more tyrannies than any other. It's been the soul food of moral dissidents the world over. More governments have burned, attacked, criticised, and forbidden this book than any other in history.'

'Your grandpa's right, Oliver.'

William smiled. 'Your girlfriend's beautiful, and she's got brains to boot.'

'All she did was agree with you, grandpa.'

'A mark of true intelligence.'

Oliver gave a silent laugh. 'OK, grandpa, you know I've been reading the Bible a lot this year—especially in preparation for my baptism. So I think I see where you're coming from. There are stories of good revolutionaries in the Bible, right?'

Grandpa William shook his head. 'No, laddie.'

'No?'

'The people of God were counter-revolutionaries.'

Oliver tilted his head. 'Huh?'

'The people of God have always recognised the ultimate authority. We're servants of the King above all kings. It's the

Samson & the Siren

world that's in rebellion—and, because of that, we're in rebellion against it.'

'Really? Like when?' Oliver asked.

'I could give ye plenty of examples,' William replied, 'but one story, in particular, comes to mind.'

'OK, let me hear it.'

'Ye sure? Might take a while if I'm to tell it properly.'

'I'd love to, grandpa, but I'm not sure Elise has the time. She has emails to send and phone calls to make.'

'Oh?' William asked, looking over at Elise.

'Yeah, there's some crazy stuf happening back in London that she's in the middle of,' Oliver said and turned to his girlfriend, 'If he gets started, there's no stopping him. I don't want you to sacrifice more time than you already have to be up here with me.'

Elise pulled out her phone, looked into it, and sighed. 'I've received two more emails on the train journey up here,' she said. 'You're right, I do need to respond to them—but I still don't know what to say. It's all so crazy and unexpected.'

'Do you want to go grab a coffee and think it through while I talk with Grandpa?'

Elise thought for a second. She knew she had significant problems to deal with back in London, but she'd come all this way to support her boyfriend and his grandpa. 'Actually, I hate conflict and need a break from it all,' she said. 'I think a story from your grandpa might be just what my stressed-out mind needs.'

'You sure?'

Elise nodded. 'Yes.'

'OK, but feel free to excuse yourself at any time.'

'I will,' she smiled, knowing that Oliver was looking out for her.

'Alright, grandpa,' Oliver said. 'Tell us this story about Christian counter-rebels.'

'Well, they wouldn't'a been called Christians back then. These were the Hebrews livin' in the ancient world. God had called the Israelis to serve him, but they'd begun worshippin' other gods and were now livin' in the shadow of a pagan government—and many of the Hebrews were no longer even tryin' to resist it. They just accepted the subservience as normal.'

'What was this pagan government called?' Oliver asked as he settled comfortably into his chair.

'A seafarin' people that had moved in from the Aegean. They were known as "Philistines".'

4

SOREK VALLEY, ISRAEL / PHILISTIA
11TH Century B.C.

'OK, REMEMBER THAT time you wondered what it would be like to wrestle freshly shorn goat covered in olive oil?' Mitinti asked.

Samson smiled. 'Yeah, even I had trouble explaining that one to my dad,' he said as they walked briskly down the dirt road.

'This is like that, only stupider.'

'How's wanting to get married stupid?'

'First, you're only twenty-one,' Mitinti said, holding up a finger.

'You forget that I'm exceptional.'

'Yeah, exceptionally thick-headed.'

'No, really,' Samson shot back. 'Listen, unlike most other guys my age, I've got money. Our business saw record sales in goats and fox traps this year.'

'Granted, you do have money on your side.' Mitinti conceded.

'Plus, a girl like Serena doesn't come around often. Look at her. She's a goddess! Can you imagine bedding her?'

Mitinti nodded. He'd imagined it many times. Serena was, after all, breathtaking in face and form. He'd considered pursuing her himself, but he knew she was out of his league. 'Yes, she is stunning. But you can't think only with your cock. Visit a prostitute if you must. Hebrew-Philisitne marriages invite problems, and you know it.'

'I don't see any problems,' Samson said with an edge of irritation. He walked faster as if to put the conversation behind him. He kicked a rock and sent it flying over the top of the hilltop thirty feet ahead, leaving a trail of dust in its wake.

'You don't see because you're choosing not to see. Look, even if your age isn't an issue, your dad will be. There's no way your parents will let you marry a Philistine.'

'Well, my dad will be easier to persuade than my mother. Sure, my parents are traditional, but you're Philistine, and they put up with you.'

'Your dad barely tolerates me. Plus, we're talking marriage here. There's no way your dad wants grandsons who grow up to be Philistine soldiers or granddaughters that wear charm bracelets to Dagon.'

20

'You're making too big a deal of this. Love is love, right?' Samson said with a shrug, 'I'll persuade my dad and, with a bit more work, my mum too. It's been twelve years since the last Hebrew-Philistine battle, right?'

'Only if you forget about the attempted Hebrew insurrections.'

'Philistine taxes and the ban on Hebrew blacksmiths don't help things either,' Samson retorted.

'I'm just a weaver. I don't make the rules. Plus, aren't taxes better than open war?'

'Perhaps. But some Philistines are still eager to take our land.'

'Yes, both sides have their zealots. I've encountered my share of radical Yahwehists.'

'Yes, there are those,' Samson said and looked over his shoulder towards Timnah. 'At least we have peace for now.'

'Thankfully.'

'Yes, thank Heaven for Egypt!'

'Shh!' Mitinti reached over to cover his friend's mouth as if he were a blaspheming child. 'Don't say that? If a Philistine soldier heard you say that, he'd kick your Hebrew behind straight into prison.'

'I'm not pro-Egyptian. All I mean is that if it weren't for your war in the South, the Philistines never would've ceased their battles with the Hebrews, we'd never have become friends, and I wouldn't be marrying Serena.'

'You're getting ahead of yourself. First, your parents need to allow you to pursue this—then her parents need to agree.'

'This is my life, not theirs.'

'Oh, so you don't need their blessing now?'

Samson thought for a moment. Even he knew what would happen if he tried to elope. 'I'll get their blessing. I'm sure I can persuade dad. Your rulers allow us to intermarry.'

'That doesn't mean every father wants his daughter to marry a Hebrew—no offence.'

'Our goat and fox trap business is at least as lucrative as her family's pottery trade. It's good business sense for him to marry his daughter off to me.'

Mitinti nodded. 'You're right. It would be a good financial move. Still, some Philistine dads are very traditional.'

'As long as the Philistines want to recruit Hebrew men to help fight your war down south, dads will have to pretend to like us.'

'Some feel this leniency compromises our strength as a people.'

'You're settlers. You should adapt to the indigenous population,' Samson said.

Mitinti laughed. 'That's rich coming from a Hebrew. Did

you guys adapt to the Canaanites when you moved into the neighbourhood?'

'That's different. Canaanites are wicked. We were right to fight them off.'

'Were you? There's division even among your people about what customs to adopt from those dogs.'

'And you? Do you have a problem with Israel?'

'You know me,' Mitinti said with a grin.

'I do. A good man is a good man. And you're a good man—which is why you'll be my best man at the wedding.'

'Me?' Mitinti asked in genuine surprise. 'Are you sure?'

'Of course. If I'm to have a Philistine bride, I must have a Philistine wedding.'

'Wow, I'm touched.'

'Don't get all mushy on me now.'

'I never realised you had so few friends.'

Samson laughed and punched his arm simultaneously. 'Moron. Look, Zorah's less than a mile away, and I still don't know what to say to my dad.'

Mitinti sighed. 'Alright. You're nuts, but I'll help. Let's rehearse something.'

The Oliver Anderson Trilogy

5

MANOAH CRINGED AT his son's words. His wife, sitting behind him, let out a sigh. Neither of them was shocked, but they weren't happy.

'So?' Samson asked. 'Whad'ya think? A spring wedding?'

Manoah looked up to meet his son's eager gaze. 'You know what I think, son,' he said soberly.

Samson's smile faded. 'I-I dunno dad. Tell me.'

'Guess if you must.'

As Samson looked for his words, Malachi, their family's chief servant, brought a bronze bowl and a pitcher of fermented goat's milk and set them both on the table between the younger and older man. Samson reached into the bowl, pulled out a dried fig. He looked back up at his father and said, 'I know you're not thrilled that Serena's a Philistine. I get that. But once you meet her, you'll forget about all that. She's a good girl.'

'Is she? What do you know about her? What's her character like?'

'Well, sh-she' Samson stuttered, realising that he and Mitinti hadn't prepared for that question. 'Her family's great. They make the best pottery in Timnah,' he responded, not answering his dad's question.

'She's from over in Timnah, huh?'

'That's right, not far at all.'

'I don't think this is a good idea. Bad things happen to men who go up to Timnah. Don't you remember what happened to the patriarch Judah when he went up there?'

'Um, yeah. I suppose I do.'

'He met Tamar dressed like a whore, and she seduced him,' Manoah said, not trying to hide the implication from his testosterone-fueled son.

'Serena's not Tamar, and I'm not Judah. So it's hardly a reason to not meet her family,' Samson protested. He looked over his father's shoulder to his mother. 'It's not too much to ask you guys to meet her parents, right?'

His mother had only listened up to this point—for which Samson was thankful. But now, her eyes flashed. 'Your father's right! The Philistines have been our oppressors. Even now, they retain control over us. Why can't you marry a good girl from the tribe of Dan—or at least an Israeli. Go back to your father's question: what's she even like, huh? Tell me about her character?'

Samson knew he couldn't change the subject quickly with his mother. He also knew it would be harder to hide that he'd never spoken directly with Serena. 'Of course, mum. Serena has a good character, a fantastic character even. The best in all of Timnah. She helps her father with his pottery business, and she has well-proportioned virtues in all the right places.'

His father gave a short and silent chuckle, but his mother wasn't amused. 'Stop thinking with your cock!'

Samson gasped. 'Mother?'

'Don't "mother" me,' she snapped back. 'You're being led by your eyes. There are deeper issues than just surface beauty. Have you ever spent time talking with her or her family?'

'Well, I—'

'How do you know she's a good girl if you haven't spent time with them? Have you said two words to her?'

'It's more that she has a solid reputation.'

'So, "no" then. You just like looking from a distance,' she said, arms crossed. 'Son, if you think we're gonna sit back and watch our only child screw up his life by chasing Philistine tail, you've got another thing coming.'

'Mum, please!' Samson pleaded, looking back towards his dad for support that wasn't forthcoming. 'It's not the same

Samson & the Siren

world as before. Their Philistine soldiers don't go around killing Israelis like they used to.'

'The only thing that's changed is Philistine tactics. They need our tax money and young men for their war, so they've changed harsh oppression for soft oppression. Behind it is the same evil. They have no love for Israel—they're only using us.'

'They simply want to cooperate.'

'What the Philistine lords call "cooperation" is tyranny. We have no choice but to go along with their rules. You think all the Philistine soldiers stationed in the valley are here to help us?'

'Those soldiers protect us from Canaanites.'

'Tyrants always claim their oppression is keeping you safe. But we wouldn't need their protection against the Canaanites if they'd allow us to have blacksmiths and raise an army of our own.'

'Look, I know the relationship with Philistia is less than ideal. But it's better than before.'

'It's sneakier than before,' she said.

Samson took a deep breath. He knew he was off track and wasn't any nearer to getting them to visit Serena's family. 'Look, mum, we've got to get along with other nations and cultures. Now I'm not trying to fix everything between Israel and Philistia. I'm just talking about one relationship with one

Philistine: me and Serena. A lot of Israeli men have taken Philistine wives—and some even from the Canaanites.'

'Those other men may have Philistine women, but you have something they don't. Those other men don't have a call on their lives as you do,' she said with a maternal finger pointed right at her son. 'You have a destiny from Heaven.'

Samson rubbed his left hand through his hair. *Yes, my calling.* He'd lost track of how many times his parents had recounted his birth story to him.

It was back when the Philistines were expanding from the sea—before their war with Egypt. His parents were young and successful in business—but without any children. As both of them were devout, they gave themselves to prayer, and Heaven answered. According to his parents, Yahweh's angel told them they'd have a son who'd rescue Israel from the Philistines. As a sign of his call, he was always to wear his hair long. They vowed they would do as the angel had said.

Samson had never seen a heavenly messenger. He'd never heard a voice from the sky either. All he had was his parent's story. He'd kept his hair long to honour them. That the girls found it attractive made it an easy vow to keep.

'Will you?' his mother asked, interrupting his thoughts.

'Huh?'

She rolled her eyes. 'Are you ever going to take it seriously?'

Samson & the Siren

Samson cleared his throat. 'Of course, mother, and I do. I just don't know why I can't serve Heaven's purposes while being married to Serena.'

His mother wasn't backing down. 'You're called to save us from the Philistines, not jump into bed with them.'

'Son,' his father interjected, 'You're a young man, I get it, you want to get married. We're just asking that you marry an Israeli.'

'Why, though? Didn't Moses teach us that God made all people's through one couple?' Samson asked rhetorically. 'Aren't we one family descended from Noah?'

'Don't excuse your horny foolishness with twisted arguments from Scripture,' his mother retorted. 'You could sell sand to a camel, but your rhetoric won't work on me. The same God who told Moses about the human family also told us not to intermarry once we came into this land.'

'It's not their fair skin,' his father interjected.

'Yes, it has nothing to do with the blood that flows through their veins,' his mother said. 'It's the gods they worship and their different morals that's the problem.'

Samson's heart beat faster as he realised his arguments weren't working. 'What if she joined Israel?' he asked before he'd even thought his words through. 'Didn't Moses say that foreigners could join us?'

His parents looked at each other, unsure of how to respond. 'Is this something she's willing to consider?' Manoah asked.

Samson knew the chances of any Philistine converting were small. A Hebrew would sometimes worship Philistine or Canaanite gods—as their pantheons were open to including Yahweh as one among many. But a Philistine renouncing their pantheon of gods and goddesses to worship Yahweh according to the Law of Moses was rare.

'It wouldn't surprise me in the least if her family were open to it,' Samson lied. 'Dad, can you at least agree just to meet her dad to discuss the possibility? What harm could come from talking? We could journey there and be back in a day.'

Manoah understood that his son had fallen for this girl and that he'd be relentless until either he got her or he got distracted by something else. He wanted to find a compromise that would keep both his son and wife happy. 'I suppose there's no harm in meeting her father and see if she would be open to converting.'

'Manoah!' his wife protested from behind.

Manoah raised his hand to quiet her. 'Heaven ordained marriage and, if the girl will embrace Israel and her God, what objection could the Law of Moses have?'

His mother crossed her arms. 'I'm suspicious of this conversion talk. Even thinking about joining yourself to a

Samson & the Siren

Philistine is a mistake. But, if your dad wants to speak with them, then I'm going with you.'

'No, mother, it's OK. We can do fine on our own.'

'Doing "fine" is why I'm worried. You might be able to twist your father's heart with your olive oil words and your honeycomb charm, but I'm your momma, and I'm going to do all I can to keep you on the right path until the day I die.'

'Here's what we'll do,' Manoah said to regain a degree of control. 'I'll send a servant over tomorrow to see if the girl's family is willing to meet us. If so, we'll arrange a date.'

Samson poured a cup of fermented milk and raised it. 'The sooner, the better.'

6

'DINNER TIME!' THE servant called. Her voice echoed off the hills and reverberated through the valley.

'No, not now!' a girl exclaimed as she stood up from within the vineyard.

A moment later, a boy came breaking through the vines. 'Ah-ha, I found you!'

'You never would've caught me if I hadn't stood.'

'Then you should've stayed hidden.'

'Don't be ridiculous, Goliath! I had to get up, it's dinner time. Come on.'

'Don't be Miss Bossy, Dee. I'll come in when I'm ready.'

'Very well, but don't blame me if dad gives you early morning milk duty again,' the girl said as she turned and headed up the hill to the house.

Goliath folded his arms and turned his back on his sister.

'Your threats won't work. Dad's still in the city.'

'Nope,' Goliath's sister replied over her shoulder. 'He got back an hour ago. I saw the horses approach the house while you were hiding.'

'OK, I'm coming,' Goliath said, taking off after his sister. 'But not because you said so.'

'Relax. I'm looking out for you.'

'I don't need a big sister to look out for me.'

'All brothers need a big sister to look out for them.'

'Hurry up, you two!' the servant called down to them. 'Your father hasn't seen you for eight days, and you're both filthy. Wash up and get to the table.'

'Yes, ma'am,' they replied. They reached the house at the summit of the hill. They dipped their hands in the water bucket and dried them on the cloth.

'Here, take this skin of wine in with you. Your father's had a stressful time in Gath.'

'How did it go?' Even at nine years of age, this Philistine daughter was aware of political tensions.

The servant sighed. 'The assembly didn't listen to him. Again. It seems there's no end in sight to this blasted war with Egypt.'

'Why won't they listen?'

33

The Oliver Anderson Trilogy

'It ain't easy to question the nation's leadership during a war. Your father's received a lot of pushback for proposing peace.'

'Poor dad.'

'Well, the company of his children, a good meal, and this skin of wine should lull his anxieties away. Now, run on in, darling.'

'Yes, ma'am,' Delilah said and dashed inside.

7

THE DISTANCE TO Timnah from Zorah is only a few miles. It's a pleasant journey that follows the Sorek river through a valley with fruitful hills on either side. The river itself served as an informal boundary between the Israeli tribe of Dan and the Philistines—but that boundary had become more fluid during Samson's young life.

This journey included Samson, his parents, and one donkey they'd brought to carry food, water, and a few presents for the girl's family. The beast also provided relief from walking whenever one of his parents found the journey too difficult.

As they came near to Timnah, his parents took a rest. At first, Samson protested as they were less than a mile from the town. But his parents insisted. As usual, his mother used the opportunity to explain why she thought meeting this Philistine family was a bad idea—a mantra that Samson was finding hard to endure.

Finally, he'd enough of his mother's nagging. He finished devouring his bread and cheese, took a swig of water, and got up for a walk with the excuse that he wanted a closer look at the surrounding vineyards. He needed the time to prepare what he'd say to Serena during their first conversation.

He walked up the hill and through the vineyards, admiring the finely cultivated Philistine grapevines. The Philistines had brought new technology and agricultural methods with them when they began colonising this land. Samson admired Philistine culture almost as much as he admired Philistine girls—they were sophisticated and enlightened. His traditional Hebrew upbringing seemed simplistic and stodgy by comparison. He hoped that the current peace between the Philistines and Israelis would continue and that marriages, like the one he hoped to start with Serena, would be an example that would better unite their peoples. The Philistines were willing to add Yahweh and local Canaanite gods to their pantheon so why couldn't Israel find ways to accept Dagon and the other Philistine deities?

Samson plucked a grape and popped it into his mouth. It was sour—the grape harvest was still a few weeks away. He lifted his head to see how far he could spit out the seeds.

That's when he saw the lion.

Samson froze. 'It can't be,' he muttered. The lion sat still, looking straight at him. Samson smiled cautiously. Lions didn't usually attack humans—preferring sheep and smaller mammals. He took a slow step backwards. 'Good cat,' he whispered.

Then the lion lept straight towards him.

When it did Samson, felt something unexpected. A weight fell on him from behind—and everything went black.

***

When Samson regained consciousness, his heart was beating uncontrollably, and blood was dripping from his hands. On the ground in front of him was a lion's body, mutilated beyond recognition. The pain of thirst caused his head to spin.

Samson looked around in confusion and terror. 'What in Heaven's name just happened?' he asked aloud. Samson looked about to see if any witnesses could explain it, but he saw no one. He turned to the lion. 'Is this the same beast?'

Samson tried to make sense of the scene. The last thing he remembered was the lion leaping at him. *But, no, there was something else. Something struck me from behind! Another lion?*

Samson's imagination raced to find a plausible explanation. 'A bigger lion, a much bigger and stronger lion, must've attacked this one—and knocked me unconscious in the process,' he reasoned out loud. He knew it wasn't a perfect explanation. There was still something about it all that didn't make sense. He'd seen lions fight. But he'd never seen a lion rip apart another lion. Not like this. He couldn't understand why the bigger, stronger lion had destroyed this one but left him untouched.

'Samson!' His father's call interrupted his thoughts.

He had no idea how long he'd been away. His first thought was what to do about his appearance. He couldn't go back to his parents—much less to Serena's family—covered in blood. How would he explain to them what happened?

He looked down at the animal's torn head. He knew he needed to get it out of the vineyard to escape notice. Samson had never seen a lion's carcass in this condition and he assumed no one else had either. He didn't want questions about a mutilated lion to surround his arrival in Timnah, so he dragged the carcass off. He tucked it away behind some rocks where it would, perhaps, be eaten by wild dogs before it received any unwanted human attention.

After hiding the beast, blood and dirt were all over Samson. He walked down the hill to the river, cautiously looking about

Samson & the Siren

to ensure he escaped his parent's notice. He jumped in the water and drank deeply. After sating his thirst, he washed the evidence off him. Once the dirt and blood were gone, he headed back to find his parents.

***

'There you are!' his mother declared as Samson approached.

'Sorry I took so long,' he said with a smile. 'I sat down to eat some grapes and fell asleep.'

'Fell asleep before meeting the girl's family?' she asked. 'I thought you'd be too full of nerves.'

'Ah, you know me, mum. I'm as cool as they get.'

'Look at you!' His father pointed at his clothes as he got closer. 'You're all wet—your hair too. What happened?'

'I was jumping on stones in the river, and I slipped and fell in,' Samson lied.

'Was that after or before the nap,' his mother asked, feeling she wasn't getting the whole story.

'That's probably not something you want to happen right before you meet this girl and her family for the first time, son,' Manoah said.

'God willing, they'll think you're a fool and send us off. Then we can be rid of this Philistine nonsense,' his mother said as Manoah loaded the remaining food and water back onto the donkey.

Samson was still trying to make sense of what happened back in the vineyard, and he had no desire to argue. 'Maybe, they will mum. Maybe.'

8

'I GUESS THE ancient Israelis were no strangers to oppression,' Oliver said to his grandpa, still sitting upright in his bed.

William nodded. 'Just because they were the chosen people doesn't mean they had it easy. On the contrary—it was very often the opposite. Early on, they were slaves in Egypt. Then, when Moses led them out after centuries of oppression, they found freedom in their homeland—but only for a while.'

'Why did God let them lose their freedom?' Oliver asked.

William looked at Elise, who had been quietly paying attention. 'Whadd'ye think, my dear? Oliver tells me that, unlike him, you had Christian parents raise ye. How would ye answer his question?'

Elise looked thoughtful for a moment before speaking. 'The Israelis were free as long as they were faithful to the God who called them and gave them the land. But, when they were

41

unfaithful and worshipped idols, God removed his protection and allowed stronger nations to oppress them. Is that it?'

'Well answered, lassie! Five hundred points to team Elise.'

Oliver smiled proudly at his girlfriend. 'Show off.'

'There's a connection between inner tyranny and outer tyranny,' William said. 'Whenever the Israelis submitted to the inner tyranny of sin and idolatry, God allowed them to experience outer tyranny of social and political oppression as a warnin'—and as a call to turn back to him.'

'But, if God allowed the Philistines to rule over Israel, does that mean Israel should've submitted to their oppressors and not fought back?'

'That, my boy, is a question the people of God have wrestled with for millennia. But, unfortunately, when to dissent and when to submit hasn't always been clear for Jews and Christians.'

'May I say something?' Elise asked gently.

William smiled. 'Of course, dear. Yer in the company of two loud Anderson men. If ye don't throw yer thoughts out with force, they'll never get heard.'

Elise blushed. She appreciated William's invitation to be bold. Throwing her thoughts into a conversation, especially with an older man she'd just met, wasn't her style. 'Has Oliver told you where my family is from?'

Samson & the Siren

William thought for a second. 'Hm, yes, I think he did. I believe he said yer parents are from Eastern Europe.'

'My family is from Czechia, yes. We moved to England when I was four. What you're talking about now—when Christians should obey the government and when they should resist—these were questions my grandparents and parents struggled with all the time when they lived under the Soviets.'

'Ah, yes, of course,' William nodded, rubbing his beard. 'The dissident church in Czechoslovakia had it rough. That Soviet government came after the church with some top-tier brain-washin'.'

Elise nodded. 'I was raised on stories of what Christians in my parents' and grandparents' generation endured. The government promised them favours and rewards if they'd be compliant citizens. It was tempting. Some Christians refused to compromise, and the police came for them. Others allowed the government to rule over how they expressed their faith and were given better jobs in return.'

'You hadn't mentioned that before,' Oliver said, surprised.

Elise smiled. 'You hadn't asked before.'

William laughed. 'Ouch! And minus five hundred points for team Oliver.'

'I didn't know to ask it,' Oliver said defensively. 'But I certainly want to hear more.'

The Oliver Anderson Trilogy

Elise smiled. 'I'm glad.'

'But, grandpa, what should people of faith do under oppressive governments? It sounds like Samson was trying to get in bed with the people in power—literally.'

'He certainly was—and he'll be in for some surprises. But, before I get back to the story, I don't want to stop Elise if she has more to share about her family under Communist rule.'

Elise shook her head. 'Not now. I'd like to hear more about Samson.'

'OK then. It seems that the encounter with the lion was just the beginning of when things began to change for him.'

9

SAMSON TOSSED AND turned in his bed. He'd fallen asleep happy about how well the day had gone with Serena and her family but, as the night progressed, shadows haunted his sleep.

He was walking outside with Serena. They were holding hands and, as they talked, Samson got lost in her brown eyes and coy smile. He leaned forward and kissed her. As Samson stepped back, Serena took hold of the tunic she was wearing and began to lift it over her head. A powerful excitement coursed through his body as he saw more and more of her skin.

When Serena finally removed her garment, she threw it over his head. He couldn't see. He fought and struggled to pull it off. But, when he managed to do so, it was no longer Serena he saw. Instead, it was the lion from the vineyard. It smiled and lept for him.

When it did, two impulses shot through him. The first was terror. But then, a moment later, another sensation came on him that he'd never felt before. It was as if a heavy emotion collapsed on him like an avalanche. The feeling was like wrath, only cleaner and more righteous than any rage of his own that he'd ever felt before. It was more than his adrenaline. It was an altogether alien rage.

The moment this force came on him, Samson leapt through the air to meet the lion with his arm outstretched. He slammed into the lion but, instead of flying backwards, the strange force drove him forward. Samson grabbed the lion's mane with his hands and pinned the fierce feline down on the ground as they landed. The beast twisted and turned to regain mastery, but a supernatural power reinforced Samson's arms and body. He slid his hands away from the lion's mane and toward its jaw. He grabbed the lions mouth, weaving his fingers away from the pointed teeth and began to pull each side apart.

How Samson knew to fight a lion with his bare hands, much less where he was getting the strength from, was a mystery. But the molten wrath he felt erupting within and around him didn't need an answer to such questions. He stretched the lion's jaw further and further apart and lifted it in the air as he did so—as if it was no more than a baby goat.

Samson & the Siren

The lion thrashed about wildly with its paws knocking Samson's body—but it might as well have been pounding and scratching a wall of iron. This lion was an enemy, and, as such, Samson knew he needed to destroy it. He stretched his hands further apart, and tissue began to tear. Fountains of blood sprouted up onto his face and in his hair. The explosive rage he felt told him there could be no letting up, no release. He saw the situation with perfect clarity: if he didn't kill this lion, it would kill him and, after him, it would devour others. He tightened his grip on the lion's mouth and, in one swift movement, tore the lion's head in half. The lion's frantic movement's stopped, and Samson dropped his enemy's body on the ground.

Samson sat up in his bed in a cold sweat, gasping for air. 'Stop, stop!' he repeated to himself. *Was that what happened yesterday?* He pondered a moment then got up to fetch some water. He drank three cups and returned to bed.

***

The time in Timnah had exceeded Samson's hopes. Serena was as charming up close as she'd been at a distance. Sitting near Samson and speaking with him only deepened his infatuation for her. Her eyes, coloured with paint in the ways that the girls of Philistia do, ignited his youthful desire.

She even made a positive impression on his parents. When they arrived, she bowed and presented them with a set of dishes she'd crafted in her father's shop. On each was the Hebrew letter for 'M' to stand for the house of Manoah. The gift even touched Samson's mother.

Serena was also impressed by Samson. She'd never spent much time with a Hebrew boy before, but she found his handsome looks, humour, charm, good physique, and evident wealth all very desirable. That Samson was only five years older than her—instead of the more typical ten to twenty years—was also a point of attraction.

There was a moment of tension when Serena's older brother expressed that he wasn't happy a Hebrew was seeking his little sister's hand in marriage. He remarked about serving pork for lunch—but his comment met with a reproachful look from his father. By contrast, Serena's younger sister was pleasant and seemed to find Samson's ethnicity a point of interest. She was only a little younger than Serena, thirteen, and Samson noticed that she was becoming every bit as lovely as her sister. *In a year or two, I could introduce her to one of my friends back in Dan,* he thought.

Towards the end of the meal, the fathers walked off to discuss finances. Expectations about dowries, future business relations between the families, and inheritance rights were issues that Israel and Philistia handled differently. Samson didn't know all that was said, but Serena's dad was supportive of their union when they returned.

Unsurprisingly, Samson's mother brought up the issue of worship. She insisted that Serena would have to join Israel and profess Israel's God if they were to marry. At first, the Philistine family responded predictably: they were happy for their daughter to add her husband's god to the ever-growing pantheon of Aegean and Canaanite deities that Philistines living in their part of the world possessed. Samson hoped his mother would drop the issue, but he had no such luck. His mother retorted that Serena would have to convert to Israel and Israel's God *only* if the marriage were to go ahead. Serena's mother wasn't happy about this. She didn't see why such exclusivity was necessary and explained that Serena already had a goddess she prayed to regularly.

Samson and Serena exchanged pained expressions. Samson didn't want to lose this girl over a question about worship. When Manoah voiced his agreement with his wife's words, an awkward silence descended upon the room. It was then that Serena's father asked if he could have a moment to speak to his daughter and wife alone. Manoah agreed, and the Philistine family got up from the table and went upstairs.

The Oliver Anderson Trilogy

Samson and his family used the time to talk. He was pleased to hear that his parents were impressed with Serena's behaviour and that her body seemed fit for producing grandchildren. It came as no surprise to Samson, however, when his mother commented, 'She *appears* sweet. But charm can be deceiving. I hope we don't move too quickly with this. Let's get to know her character first.'

Moving quickly was, of course, precisely what Samson's horny body wanted to do. Yes, he wanted to know her better. But he wanted to get to know her better naked—a value that he doubted his mother shared.

It wasn't long before Serena's family came back down and sat at the table. They exchanged glances, and her father cleared his throat. 'We've talked and decided that Serena can convert to Israel and Israel's God if your family insists upon it.'

Samson's face beamed, and Manoah gave a modest nod to his wife. She smiled but, but her eyes still reflected suspicion. Serena winked at Samson, and he got lost once again in her mysterious eyes.

Everything went smoothly from then onwards. The family sipped wine while Samson and Serena had the chance to sit alone while the parents stepped into the next room. Once they had some privacy, Samson gushed about how beautiful he found Serena to be. Serena smiled, listened, and responded that

Samson & the Siren

she also found Samson attractive and how she looked forward to them being married so that she could give herself to him entirely—a thought that unleashed a storm of hormones within the young man.

By the time they'd finished, it was getting late in the afternoon, and Manoah announced that they must leave if they were to get back to Zorah before dark. Serena's father asked if the engagement between their children was now formal. Samson said 'Yes' at the exact moment his mother said 'No'. It was Manoah that clarified the situation. 'What we mean is that we are pleased with this discussion and that we are informally inclined. But it is not the tradition of our people to rush into an engagement. We will discuss it as a family and, at the end of one week, will propose marriage formally—should we decide to go ahead.'

Serena's dad, perhaps wanting to maintain an equal sense of honour, responded, 'Well, if you do, then we will take one week to consider your proposal and decide if we wish to accept.'

'I would expect nothing less from such a fine family as yours,' Manoah said as he bowed—a comment which pleased the Philistines.

The walk back home was a mixture of emotions. Samson's mother expressed more than once she thought things were going too quickly. Manoah clarified for both of them that they had a whole week to discuss and pray about the matter. And Samson, who was still a virgin, could think about little else than undressing and making love to Serena. Only when they passed the spot where they had taken the food and water break did Samson remember the bizarre encounter with the lion, only to forget about it a minute later.

And it stayed forgotten—until he fell asleep.

10

'ARE YOU TWO having fun yet?' Mitinti shouted over the music as he approached Samson and Serena. A large group of young men followed behind him.

Samson turned to his friend, his arm around his new bride and a cup of wine in his free hand. 'We're not bad for the first day—though I trust it will get even better as the week progresses,' he said.

'And how are you, my lady?' Mitinti asked Serena as he leaned in to kiss her cheek.

Serena grinned. 'I'm just fine. I'm especially enjoying the musicians. Did you help Samson find them?'

'I did indeed, my dear.'

Samson lifted his eyes to the group following behind his friend. 'Mitinti, who are all these guys with you?'

'It's the men for your entourage. The ones I told you about.'

Samson's eyes grew wide. 'All of them? How many are there?'

'Thirty. Same as every Philistine wedding.'

'Thirty? That's far more than at Hebrew weddings. Who are they?'

'Just some friends of mine.'

'Mitinti, I've known you for eight years. You don't have thirty friends. The reason you and I hang out together is that no one else will have us.'

Mitinti shrugged his shoulders. 'OK, so maybe "friends" is too strong a word. I promised them food, so they came. Regardless, you need them.'

'Do I?'

'Samson, my love,' Serena cut in, 'Mitiniti's right. Every man getting married must have thirty in his entourage. It's our custom.'

'It's not my custom.'

'Come now. You said we could do this the Philistine way. You wouldn't disappoint me on my wedding week, would you?' she asked and pouted her lips.

'Of course not, my dear,' he replied, not wanting to let his bride down. 'But that's thirty more mouths to feed. Between them and all the extended Philistine family showing up, I'm gonna have to put some more orders in for the feast.'

'But you, I mean "we", are well off, aren't we, my love?'

'I—we—do have the money for it… but still.'

'Well, it's only twenty-nine more,' Mitinti grinned. 'I'm the thirtieth.'

'Yes, but you eat like a pig. It'll take a lot to fill your belly.'

Mitinti feigned offence. 'You're calling me fat?'

'I know five fat people, Mitinti. And you're three of them.'

Serena rolled her eyes and laughed. 'Men! You're so terrible to each other. But, my love, if our Philistine wedding is too big and expensive for you, perhaps I could ask my father to—'

'No,' Samson said, cutting her off. 'In Hebrew culture, it's the groom that prepares the wedding feast and the place of residence for his bride. My parents haven't even helped. They've just been discussing legal matters with your parents while I've gotten all this ready. If a Hebrew man can't afford his wedding, how's he supposed to afford a wife?'

'Of course, honey, I understand,' Serena said and patted her groom's cheek. 'Mitinti, why don't you take my husband's entourage to the wine tent and get them some drinks?'

'As you wish,' he said and blew her a kiss. He turned and faced the group behind him. 'Come on, fellas. To the wine tent!' he shouted to grunts of approval, and off they went.

'Excuse him,' Samson said. 'He's a bit of a flirt.'

Serena grinned. 'Did he get it from you, or did you get it from him?'

'Well, I—'

'Serena!' a woman's voice interrupted. The couple turned to see a young family headed towards them. The woman looked to be in her late twenties, and her husband seemed about forty. Both were dressed well in ways that spoke of their high class.

'Remember me?' the woman asked with a big smile.

Serena stared at her with a puzzled look. Then a light flashed through her eyes. 'Wait, cousin Marna?'

'Yes!' the woman exclaimed, and the two women embraced.

'Wow!' Serena exclaimed. I haven't seen you since your wedding, what is it, ten years ago? You look great.'

'Thank you and, yes, it's been just over a decade,' Marna replied and turned to Samson. 'Greetings, you must be Serena's Hebrew Husband.'

'Guilty as charged. But I think I'm Serena's only husband,' he replied with a hint of defensive sarcasm. 'Call me Samson.'

'Welcome to the Philistine family,' Marna replied. 'This is my husband, Phicol.' The men exchanged customary salutes. 'I'm the cousin of Serena's cousin—whatever that makes us.'

A young girl reached out from behind Marna and touched Serena's dress. 'Well, greetings, young lady,' Serena responded, bending down to the girl. 'Do you like my dress?'

The girl smiled. 'You're pretty.'

'Why, thank you. I think you're pretty too.' Serena looked up to her cousin. 'I guess these are yours.'

'Yes, of course, let me introduce them properly,' Marna said, placing her hand on the girl and pulling a small boy out from behind her. 'This Goliath and his big sister, Delilah.'

'It's nice to meet you both.'

'Here,' Phicol said. 'We've brought you two gifts,' he stepped forward and handed one linen-wrapped gift to Serena and one to Samson. Serena unwrapped hers and held up a necklace.

'Marna, thank you, it's lovely. And such a unique design!'

Samson inspected his gift. It was a clay jar filled with honey—lighter honey than the dark pine honey the local bees produced.

'Hope you like them,' Marna said. 'They're both Egyptian.'

'Shh,' Phicol interrupted his wife. 'There's no need to mention where they come from.'

Marna bit her bottom lip. 'Sorry, I forget.'

Samson gave Phicol a sceptical look, 'Don't you guys have an embargo on Egyptian goods at the moment?'

'Not everyone in these parts appreciates the good produce and craftsmanship from down south,' he said in a low voice. 'Please, forget about where they came from. Just enjoy.'

'Of course, we will,' Samson replied, curious who this new relative of his might be.

'Come,' Marna said, 'This couple has only just begun their wedding week. Let's let them welcome others.'

'Yes, my love, I hear the wine table calling us now.' And with that, they walked with their children towards the tent.

'They were nice,' Serena remarked.

'Yes, I'd say so. How well do you know them?'

'Not well. Marna's a distant relative. I didn't expect they'd come—but they don't live too far away. My parents must've invited them.'

'Interesting folks.'

'Yes, and I love this necklace,' Serena said and placed one hand on her new husband's cheek. 'I might wear it this evening when we spend our first night together—that and nothing else.'

Samson grinned. 'I'm no fashion expert, but I think the necklace might look great with an outfit like that.'

'Why don't you take the necklace along with the honey back to our tent? I'm sure we can find some uses for the honey as well.'

Samson loved how Philistine girls talked. 'Whatever you say,' he replied, his grin now stretching ear to ear.

'Now that's my good Hebrew. Hurry along. We have many more relatives and family friends to greet.'

'Of course,' Samson replied and rushed off to the tent. His mind spun as he imagined all that their first night together

Samson & the Siren

might involve. But that came to a halt when Samson looked down at the honey. Glancing at it shot his mind back four days to when he'd travelled down with his parents from Zorah.

***

It had been a fine Spring day for travelling but, when they got near Timnah, Samson remembered the strange incident with the lion that had happened a few months previous. Curiosity overtook him, and he asked his parents if they could have a rest.

'Now who's getting old?' his father teased him.

After eating a bit, Samson said, 'I need to piss.'

'Samson.'

'I meant "pee". Sorry mother,' he replied and rose up and head for the hills. His bladder was only moderately full—he wanted to see if the lion's carcass was still where he left it. He wanted to verify that the whole incident hadn't been a strange hallucination or dream.

But the lion was still there—though much of the flesh had decayed. At first, the sight of the carcass repulsed him. But, as he leaned in for a closer inspection, he heard a buzzing all about the lion's body. As he looked closer, he saw that the buzzing wasn't coming from flies as one would typically expect. Instead, bees were flying in and out of the skeletal remains.

Samson cautiously approached and saw that the bees had built a hive inside the lion's body. Samson got low to the ground—he had never seen such a thing. Honey was oozing out onto the rock around the carcass. Samson stretched out his finger to touch it and brought the stick goodness to his mouth. *Delicious!* He was amazed both by the richness of the honey and how it came from such an ugly source. "What a contrast!" He remarked.

Emboldened by his success in getting a small taste, Samson reached closer and bent a piece of comb off the hive. Then, he crawled away from the lion with his treasure in hand. When he arrived back to where his parents were waiting, he shared the honey with them.

'Where'd you find this?' his mother asked.

'There was hive up in the trees,' Samson said casually. 'A piece of comb had fallen onto the ground.'

'A fortunate discovery. This is good honey!' his father said, enjoying the treat. 'Hopefully a sign of Heaven's blessing on your upcoming wedding week.'

'Yes, hopefully,' Samson said as they headed towards town.

***

That was four days ago. Now Samson was standing in his tent, holding his pot of Egyptian honey and staring out onto the sunny hills circling the Sorek valley. 'Yes, father, he muttered to himself, 'Maybe the honey was a sign—but is it one of Heaven's blessing?'

60

11

SAMSON'S HAND TREMBLED in the pale, flickering light of the lamp. His body was tense, and his breath was laboured. The week that had begun so wonderfully had spiralled into a nightmare.

He stood in his tent, scared and confused. 'What do I do now?' he asked—half to himself and half as a prayer.

Samson turned as someone entered his tent. It was his mother. She walked up to him without saying a word and placed her hand on his back.

'Mum, h-how did you know?' Samson stuttered.

'Know what? I saw you run in here, and it seemed you were upset.'

He sighed. 'Yes. You saw right.'

'Am I right in thinking that, whatever is the matter, it has been building for a few days?'

Samson paused before answering. 'You've always been… observant.'

'You're my only child. What else should I pay attention to?'

'It's this week. It-it hasn't—'

'You're a married man now, son,' she interrupted. 'You don't have to tell me anything anymore.'

'But, it's not what I'd imagined. The week started as Heaven, and it's ended as hell.'

'I'm so sorry,' she said, taking his hand. 'I'm not sure what I can do but, if there is, tell me.'

'I'm angry… angrier than I remember being in a long time. Look, my body is shaking, and I don't know how to control it.'

His mother looked at him with the type of concern that only a mother can and squeezed his hand. 'I don't know if I've ever seen you this way. Sit down and tell me about it,' she said. They sat down on two pillows in the middle of the tent. His mother lit another lamp that was beside them.

'It's Serena. And the Philistines,' Samson said. 'All of them. Even Mitinti.'

'Mitinti, your friend?' his mother asked. 'By Heaven, what's the matter?'

'The first two days went well. I took Serena to my tent and, well, it was wonderful.'

'These are not details a man needs to tell his mother.'

'No, I know. I just mean it was fine. It was on day three the problems began. I could tell by then that some of the Philistine men Mitinti had found weren't happy that a beautiful Philistine girl was marrying a Hebrew. The first two days, they'd kept their thoughts to themselves but, after they'd drunken enough of my wine and eaten my food, the truth began slipping out. These strangers teased me—at my own wedding!'

'Son, I'm sorry.'

'I thought those days were over… that Philistines and Hebrew could be friends. I'd heard jokes before—I can take Hebrew jokes. But this was mocking—by men that I was feeding.'

'Did you say something to them?'

'My pride was hurt, so I challenged them with a riddle.'

'You used riddles? On Philistines?'

'Yes, and I placed a large bet on it.'

'Oh, no,' she said, rubbing her forehead. 'This doesn't sound good. How much?'

'Thirty suits of clothes.'

'Thirty! Son, we might have money, but thirty is—'

'I was confident I could win.'

'Well, tell me. Which riddle did you use?'

The Oliver Anderson Trilogy

'It wasn't one you've heard before, mum.'

She smiled, 'How do you know which ones I've heard before, huh?' she said, giving him a smile and a tap on the shoulder. 'I'm an old woman and have heard every riddle Israel has produced.'

'It was one I made up.'

'You used a made-up riddle for a thirty suit wager? Heaven help us! Since when have you made up riddles, anyway?'

'Since this week,' he smiled. The familiarity of talking with his mother was calming him.

'Well, let me hear it.'

Samson cleared his throat. 'Out of the eater came something to eat. Out of the strong came something sweet.'

'Eat? Sweet? What's this riddle of yours?'

'Just something I've been thinking about,' Samson replied, having no desire to explain about the lion. Anyway, the point is, the Philistines couldn't guess the answer. They flooded me with guesses, but they were nowhere near correct.'

'Hm. Well, I see why. It's like nothing I've heard before.'

'The next day, Serena began to ask me about it. She wanted to know the answer.'

'Did you tell her?'

'No.'

'Why not? She's your wife now.'

'I didn't because, well... I'm not sure why.'

'Did you not trust her?'

'Well, of course, I-I—' Samson began, but as he thought it through, he realised that perhaps he had doubted her. 'Maybe I didn't trust her,' he confessed.

'It's good to marry someone we love. It's better to marry someone we trust.'

Samson sat in silence. 'Yes. You've told me that before. Now I see just how true those words are.'

'Well, what happened?'

'She didn't respect my decision not to tell her. She nagged me for three days—with each day worse than the day before. We haven't been back to bed since day two of this week.'

'I don't need—'

'I know, no details. But, the point is, Serena insisted on being miserable unless I told her. She cried and pouted and refused any intimacy with me.'

'Is that why you're so angry?'

'That's just a part. It's what happened next. I finally told Serena the answer, but only after she swore secrecy.'

'And?'

65

'An hour later, the thirty men approached me with the answer I'd given Serena.'

His mother looked down at the tent floor and sighed. 'Oh, son.'

'They stood there, laughing at me,' Samson said, his jaw tightening and his voice rising. 'They mocked me at my own wedding!'

'Son, I'm so sorry.'

His fists clenched, and he began to growl as much as speak. 'Even Mitinti was there. Mitinti! No, he wasn't laughing at me openly like the others, but he was drunk enough on my wine to find the whole thing amusing—I could see it in his Philistine eyes!'

'Son, please calm down,' his mother said, reaching out to place her hand on his shoulder. 'God can bring good even out of this. There is always some good we can find to be thankful for.'

He batted her hand away. 'No! There will be no calming down,' he cried, leaping to his feet. 'There will be no searching for something good in this. I may like jokes, but I am not a joke. I've honoured the Philistines, and this is how they repay me. I will not be mocked—certainly not on my wedding week.'

'Son, why don't I get your father,' she said, rising to her feet too. 'Perhaps we can have a good sleep and, in the morning, we'll speak with Serena's parents and—'

'Serena? That lying whore? I'll be damned if I'm ever speaking to her or her family again.'

'Son, you're scaring me,' his mother said as Samson turned from her and headed out of the tent.

'I'm sorry, mother. I must go.'

'Stop!' she commanded. Samson froze.

'It was you who wanted to marry a Philistine. It was you who wanted to rush the wedding before we could know her character. Now you must own your choices. You may have a wife of poor character—but you must live with that. You can't run away from bad choices.'

Samson nodded respectfully to his mother. But, when he looked up at her, she saw his eyes aflame. 'You're right. I must be responsible. I was a boy—now I'll be a man. I'll run, but it won't be away from my problems. I'll go, but I'll be back.'

'What are you talking about?'

'Men gotta keep their word—or this world falls apart,' he said as he headed out the tent.

'Where are you going?' she shouted.

The Oliver Anderson Trilogy

Samson turned to face his mother, and fear shot through her when she saw his eyes—they were wild like those of a beast. 'To get thirty suits of clothes,' he growled and ran off into the trees of the Sorek valley.

As he ran down the hill, a power came on him from behind. He bolted through the mountains towards the sea and ran with a ferocity that he'd never known. It was like a sprint—only he did not weary as the minutes and miles went by.

Finally, after two hours of running without breaking his stride, he approached the Philistine harbour city of Ashkelon. A few torches lit the open gate where a group of men stood. Samson's speed did not let up.

'Stop! Identify yourself,' a man from the group shouted, placing his hand on the hilt of his sword. The Philistine men also turned and focused their attention on the shadow hurtling towards them.

'Who is it?' one called out.

'What is it?' asked another.

A moment before Samson reached them, just as the torchlight allowed him to see their faces, a question shot through his rage possessed mind. 'What in Heaven's name am I about to do?' A yell from deep within erupted from his mouth. He lept through the air towards the group—and everything went black.

12

'DO YOU FEEL as bad as you look?' Manoah asked his son.

'I dunno,' Samson replied, lifting his gaze from the bread and goat's cheese on his plate. 'How do I look?'

'Like pig filth.'

'That bad?'

'The resemblance is uncanny,' his father quipped with a smile as he sat across from him. 'Look, son, you can't continue like this. I appreciate how you've thrown yourself into work with the goats, the traps, and the fox skins—it's been a record few months—but your mother and I worry for you. I don't think I've seen you smile twice since the wedding.'

'It was a mistake—and I don't know how to fix it.'

'Well, you could get your wife and bring her back with you from Timnah. You did love her once, didn't you?'

Samson & the Siren

'Did I? I was attracted to her. I thought that would translate into love.'

'But you've married her. She's your wife. You can't leave her at her father's house forever.'

'She hurt me, dad. She betrayed me to those idiots Mitinti found.'

'You don't think your mother has ever said or done anything that's hurt me?'

Samson smiled. 'Yeah, mum has a feisty way about her sometimes. But, even if she says something hurtful, you still trust her, don't you?'

'Yes, I do,' Manoah confessed. 'Trust is the bedrock of marriage.'

'I don't trust Serena.'

'A good marriage isn't one in which the two people never hurt each other. It's one where they learn to forgive. We all come into marriage far more selfish than we realise—then we spend our lives learning how to give and receive forgiveness.'

'It was more than an accidental hurt. Serena manipulated me with her nagging to get the answer to my riddle—then she gave it to her Philistine friends.'

'I'll admit, that looks bad. But have you asked Serena for her side of the story? Maybe there are other factors you're unaware of. Maybe the last four months has given her time to regret what she did. How would you know unless you talk with her?'

Samson knew he was right. But, though he was honest with his dad, he wasn't sharing everything. Yes, his anger at his new wife was one of the reasons he'd left her in Timnah.

But there was more.

That night in Ashkelon haunted him. He'd killed thirty men for their clothes with his bare hands. The images of his fists smashing skulls and his hands ripping off the arms and legs of his adversaries was clear in his mind. It wasn't so much the violence that bothered him. It was the alien force that empowered it all that he didn't understand.

He'd left no witnesses. He washed the bloody clothes in the river before dropping them off at the tents of his thirty Philistine wedding companions—thus keeping his word. But he knew what had happened, and that was enough for him to stay away from Philistia.

'OK,' Samson replied, coming out of his thoughts.

'OK, what?' his dad asked.

'I'll do it. I'll head up to Timnah and see her today. Maybe, if it goes well, she'll even return with me.'

Manoah smiled. 'Glad to hear it. Take a goat with you as a gift.'

'I will.'

The walk to Timnah wasn't long. The early autumn sun was still hot but not overbearing. This time, Samson didn't have his elderly parents with him to slow his journey. His only companion on this trip was the goat he draped over his shoulders.

As he walked, his mood improved, and he allowed himself to hope. He remembered all he'd loved about Serena: her sophistication, he painted eyes, and the first couple of nights they'd shared during their wedding week. The pleasant memories quickened his pace, and he determined to make love to her before attempting to convince her to return with him.

By the time he arrived in Timnah, he was so optimistic and focused on seeing Serena that he simply walked into their courtyard and announced, 'I'm here for my wife!'

A slave was the first to see him. When he did so, he turned and rushed off, leaving Samson standing there with the goat. A moment later, Serena's father entered the courtyard with a look of surprise.

'Samson? What brings you here?'

'I'm here for my wife,' he replied, unsure why the old man should be so shocked to see him. 'Here, I've brought a young goat as a gift for your family. I should have come back for Serena earlier—I just had a lot to think about.'

'Is that how they do it in Israel?'

'Whaddya mean? Is the gift of a goat unusual?'

'No, I mean leaving a bride at her father's house for four months and expecting to come back for her,' He retorted. 'Is that something you Hebrews do?'

Samson stiffened at his father-in-law's cold greeting. 'I apologise. Leaving a bride at her father's house isn't normal in Israel either. I dunno if she told you, but we got into a big fight at the end of our wedding week. That's why I left.'

'Oh, and now you're here to fix it, are you?' her dad asked, not hiding his scorn.

Samson shrugged. 'Better late than never?'

'Maybe that's how they do things in Israel, but here it's different. If a husband leaves his wife, as you did, she's a free woman. Serena is no longer available to you.'

'What? No longer available? No, she's my wife! I'm here to take her back home with me.'

'Go back to your goat-home. Serena's found another man—a Philistine. He's moved in with us and has proved to be an economically valuable part of the family.'

Samson's mouth dropped. 'My wife?'

Her father grinned. 'I assumed, since you left, you didn't want her. Her new boyfriend was only too eager.'

Samson & the Siren

Samson's heart raced. His fists tightened, and his teeth grated. 'I will see her now!' He ran into the house. He flew up the stairs and headed to Serena's bedroom, determined to reclaim his wife. When he got to her door, he kicked it open.

Someone sat up in the bed. 'Hey, darling, did you remember to get... Samson?'

Samson froze as he looked at the naked body in front of him. 'Mitinti?'

13

'UH, YEAH, IT'S me,' Mitinti said uneasily. 'What are you doing here?'

'I should ask you that question.'

'Well, isn't it obvious? After you left Serena, she was alone, and I comforted her as a friend. To my surprise, she expressed interest. I couldn't exactly say no to a girl like her. You understand, right?'

'I understand that you're sleeping with my wife.'

'When you say it like that, it sounds as if you think this is wrong. This won't be an issue, will it?'

'An issue? I was your best friend!' Samson spun and punched a hole into the wall behind him.

'Whoa! Calm down, buddy. You were my best *Hebrew* friend—and you guys have odd ideas about sex and marriage. If

76

you want to stay the night and sleep with Serena, I don't mind sharing her with you.'

'You're telling me I can share my wife with you?'

Mitinti rolled his eyes. 'Stop being so Hebrew about this.'

'Hebrew? Since when did being Hebrew ever—'

'Samson!' a familiar voice interrupted. Samson turned to see Serena standing half-naked, holding two cups of wine. 'What are you doing in my room?'

Samson choked in amazement. 'Serena, I'm your husband! Your room is my room.'

'You *were* my husband—for all of five minutes.'

'You betrayed me, we argued, and I left... for a bit.'

'You left four months ago!'

'That doesn't change that we're married.'

'Maybe to you, it doesn't. But in Philistia, I'm free to give myself to whomever I wish after such abandonment.'

'That's not how things should be!' Samson lifted his fist to strike.

'Stop, Samson!' It was Serena's father with her younger sister standing behind him. 'What are you doing to my house?' he asked wide-eyed, pointing to the hole in the wall.

'Who cares about the wall! You gave my wife to Mitinti.'

'Didn't you hear me, boy?

'Boy?'

'Yeah, "boy". You didn't want her, remember?'

'We were married.'

He laughed. 'I can see we're not going to convince you of your unreasonableness. But, look, if it stops you punching holes in my house, you could always take her sister here. She's pretty, wouldn't you say?' he said, pushing his youngest daughter to the centre of the room.

'Her sister?' Samson asked.

'She just turned fourteen—she's of age now. Why don't you take her for the night?' Serena's sister looked up at Samson and smiled.

'You gave my wife to my friend, and you think giving me her little sister fixes this? That's sick!.'

'Don't make a big deal out of this, Samson,' Serena said, placing her hand on his arm. 'What's the point of being so angry?'

'You can have a foursome for all I care,' her father replied. 'Just don't break my house.'

'But I—'

'Come on, buddy,' Mitinti said. 'Perhaps we acted hastily, but that's in the past. Let's forget about it and have a good time.'

Suddenly, Samson felt himself to be of two minds. One part of him wanted to drink his anger away with a pitcher of wine and have a wild night. But the other part of him was offended on behalf of his people. Perhaps for the first time, he saw just how opposed a Philistine life was to a Hebrew one. He'd been so busy telling other Hebrews that the Philistines' lighter skin and shaved beards didn't matter that he'd overlooked differences that did—differences of behaviour and codes of honour.

He had a choice before him, and he knew that this choice would determine the course of his life. Would he be a Hebrew or a Philistine? For a long time, he'd comfortably had a foot in each world. However, he now faced a chasm too wide to straddle—and felt unprepared to make his choice.

Then, something he'd once heard shot through his mind. 'A man should not have a woman and her sister,' Samson said, unsure if he was speaking to himself or the others in the room.

'Oh?' Mitinti asked mockingly. 'Where did you get that from?'

'Um, the Law of Moses.'

'Never heard you quote that before. Have you become one of those strict Yahwehists you used to make fun of?'

Samson felt wrath building, but he wasn't out of control. Not yet, but soon. He took a deep breath and looked around the room. 'As a young man, I was looked down on by our traditionalists for being too friendly with Philistines. I believed that, since our people weren't at war, we could learn from each other. But now I see your attitude. You didn't stop fighting us because you respect us. You stopped fighting us because you want to use us.'

Mitinti chuckled. 'Come on, Sammy. Enough with the Hebrew melodrama. Let's get drunk and enjoy these girls.'

Samson's eyes burned at his friend. 'The last time I attacked Philistines, I felt remorse for it—'

'Huh? Attack? When did you ever attack Philistines?' their father asked.

Samson ignored the question. 'I felt remorse before. But never again.' He looked at Serena one last time. 'I did love you. Or, maybe it's more true to say that I loved myself through you. Either way, it's a mistake I'll not make again.' Then he turned and fled the room, shoving the father out of the way as he fled.

***

When Samson got home that night, he called out their chief servant, Malachi. 'How many foxes do we have waiting to be skinned?'

'Sixty, sir,' he replied.

'That's not enough for what I need.'

'Not enough? What would you need so many for?'

'Come, Malachi. Bring all the traps we have in store. Tonight we're gonna hunt!'

Samson & the Siren

14

SOLDIERS HAD FILLED the house and the courtyard, in what they had assumed was a routine security check, when the general unexpectedly arrived. His arrival ended all jesting and caused them to stand soberly, if not fearfully, at attention as he strode past, surveying the scene. 'A potter's house. One of above-average means,' he remarked, stroking his midnight-black goatee.

He walked inside, looked around, and noted the large, well-decorated reception room. The father and other family members were individually tied up and gagged in the centre of the room, surrounded by four soldiers. The general approached them and looked closely at each one before sitting down on a large pillow.

'Well, I must say, you don't have the look of revolutionaries. Well? What do you have to say for yourselves?'

The terrified father tried to speak but was unable. The general pointed, and a soldier removed his gag. 'P-please, sir, we're unaware of what crimes condemn us. B-but, whatever they may be, I assure you of our innocence.'

The general smiled. In his experience, there were no genuinely innocent men—just those who were less guilty than others. 'You seem sincere, my good potter,' he responded to the man whose eyes lit up as if receiving good news. 'But I'm afraid sincerity is not the same as innocence. Tell me, do you know who I am?'

The man shook his head and looked down, 'No, sir.'

'No? Well, maybe you've heard of me. My name is Achish, General of National Safety.'

The introduction caused the father to tremble. 'P-please, sir. We've done nothing wr-rong.'

'Is that right' Achish asked. 'Tell me, are you aware of the fields that were set on fire yesterday?'

'Y-yes, sir. Everyone has heard of the tragedy.'

'And have you heard who burnt them down?'

'N-no, sir. Canaanite insurrectionists?'

'That's what we assumed at first. But it would seem that Hebrew, not Canaanite, hands committed this arson.'

The man's eyes exploded to half the size of his face. 'It was a Hebrew?'

'Yes. And, from what our intelligence can gather, the Hebrew who committed this act was in your house earlier that same day. Is that right?'

This information struck him like a blow to the gut. 'We, we had S-Samson here.'

'Samson, yes. That's his name. Witnesses say he left your home in a passion. Tell me, what did you talk about that inspired him to attack our fields? Are you in the pay of Egypt?'

'Egypt? No, sir! We quarrelled with Samson, and he left angry.'

'So you offended a Hebrew to such a degree—one who has, to our knowledge, never been guilty of anti-Philistine sentiment—that he does severe damage to our crops. What, in the name of Dagon, did you do to this fellow?'

The potter looked over at his daughter. 'N-nothing. We did nothing. It was just a minor disagreement.'

Achish said nothing but reached to his belt and drew his dagger. Its sharp blade glistened in the sunlight that flooded the room from the East facing window. The general gently ran his finger along the edge of it, appreciating its razor-sharp edge. He looked back down at the man. 'Why don't you think again.'

Serena's father got the message and looked down. 'I-I gave his wife away. She was my daughter, and I gave her to another man.'

83

'You took your daughter back from this Hebrew after she'd married him?'

'Y-yes, sir,' he said, his body now visibly quaking.

'So, when the Philistine Lords declare that we're to be on good terms with the Hebrews so that we can divert our military attention to Egypt, you foolishly rob a Hebrew of his wife? Is that what you've done?' The father was silent and stared at the ground. 'You know, potter, if someone stole one of my wives and gave her to another man, I'd be angry too.'

'We're sorry, sir. We didn't realise he'd respond this way.'

'That's because you're stupid, my dear potter,' Achish quipped as he walked over to Serena. 'So, you must be the little whore. Is that right?' Serena nodded her head and diverted her gaze in fear. 'Well, you are lovely. If you were mine, I wouldn't want to share you either. Tell me, to whom did your father give you?' Serena turned her eyes towards Mitinti, who was also bound and gagged near her sister. 'Ah, I see—a lover-boy.'

'Please, have mercy on my daughters and me. We didn't know what Samson was capable of,' the father pleaded.

'A man can be capable of a lot when you steal his wife away.'

A soldier approached Achish and handed him two items. 'Have a look at these, sir. We found the necklace in the daughter's room and the pot in the kitchen.'

Samson & the Siren

Achish looked closely at them. 'Well, potter, it looks like there's more to this story—an expensive piece of Egyptian jewellery and some Egyptian honey in a jar bearing the seal of Pharoah Rameses. Naturally, the Egyptians would like nothing more than for us to fight the Hebrews again. Do you mind explaining how you came into possession of these goods? Was it payment of some kind?' The father glanced at his daughter and then back to the ground. Achish turned to Serena. He knelt beside her, pulled out her gag, grabbed her hair, and lifted her gaze from off the floor. 'They found the jewellery in your room. How did it get there?'

Serena thought about Marna. 'I-I forget,' she replied.

'Ah, you forget, do you?' Achish asked as he tightened his grip on her hair. 'You know, my dear, as the General of National Safety, I've developed certain ways to help people remember. Would you like me to show you some of them?'

Serena bit her lip.

'You see these soldiers? I have fifty of them right here at my command. All I have to do is give the word, and they'll happily take turns raping every orifice in your body.'

Serena looked into the cold eyes in front of her and knew he spoke the truth. Her body spasmed in terror as she said, 'My cousins! My cousins gave them to me as a wedding gift.'

'Your wedding to Samson?'

'Yes.'

'Hm, so there is some connection. Glad to see your memory is returning,' Achish purred, rubbing his hands through her hair. 'Tell me, what are the names of these cousins?'

Serena looked over to her father. He nodded. 'Marna and her husband, Phicol. I think they live in the Sorek, but I've never been to their house.'

'Phicol from the Sorek? Would he, by chance, be the same Phicol who sits in the national assembly?'

'I-I don't know. I know they have money, and I've heard he's a man of some importance—b-but I don't know the details,' Serena said, her voice trembling.

'I believe you have told me everything I need to know.'

'P-please sir,' she said. 'Please don't send your soldiers on me.'

Achish smiled. 'Don't worry your faithless tits off, my dear. I won't send them on you,' he said. Serena sighed in relief. Then, he pointed to the four soldiers standing in the room. 'You, you, you, and you.'

'Yes, sir!' they cried in unison.

'Take the girl and her father out into the courtyard and burn them to death.'

'Yes, sir!' the guards replied and grabbed them both.

Samson & the Siren

Cries of horror filled the room. Achish followed the soldiers outside. There was no show or drama. They were thrown, still bound with ropes, onto the tiled ground of the courtyard. One soldier doused them with liquid from a leather container, and another extended a torch. They lit up instantly.

Their screams, along with the black smoke, filled the air. The father yelled for half a minute, and then his voice weakened and began to fade as the flames consumed his flesh. It took longer for the fire to devour Serena. Her screams came back and forth like waves for nearly two minutes—and then went out with a gasping whimper. No one who heard her would ever forget it.

Achish turned to face the neighbourhood. 'Let this be a lesson to all!' he cried. 'Anyone found guilty of collaborating with the Egyptians or disturbing our peace with the Hebrews will be considered an enemy! We cannot risk the good of the community for personal disputes. We must stay safe!'

Then, turning to one of his officers, he said, 'Take ten men, find out where this Samson lives. I want him captured. Kill anyone who stands in your way. I'll take the rest and search the home of Phicol, the assemblyman. If the pot of honey and jewellery originated from him, then he has some explaining to do. If he's guilty of treason with Egypt, well, we'll deal with that accordingly.'

The Oliver Anderson Trilogy

15

SAMSON WIGGLED UNCOMFORTABLY on the cave floor. The words of Caleb, the Judean elder, annoyed him. The last few days were beginning to blur together due to lack of sleep, and the conversation he was having now was awkward.

'I'm sorry, Samson. Your parents are people of respect, but the Philistines are still our overlords. We cannot afford to lose our peace with them.'

'They bully you into handing me over—and you call peace?'

'You killed five of their soldiers and injured five more. And for what?'

'They killed my wife and attacked me. I simply fought back. It was self-defence.'

'I'm sorry about your wife,' Caleb said sincerely. 'How you managed to take out ten Philistine soldiers all alone, I have no idea. All I know is that we have several hundred of them now in

Lehi demanding we hand you over or else they will end our peace agreement.'

'This isn't peace!' Samson yelled, losing his temper. 'If I've committed a crime, then try me in an Israeli court.'

'I'd like to, son,' Caleb said sympathetically, rubbing his long grey beard. 'But I have no choice. I'm responsible for the well-being of Judean men, women, and children. I can't allow open war with Philistia again.'

'They tax us, recruit our men for their wars, forbid us blacksmiths and the ability to defend ourselves. This is oppression and tyranny—not peace.'

'It's better than the open killing. You're too young to remember what that was like.'

Samson sighed. He'd heard enough stories from his parents to know that the older man spoke some truth. He felt sorry for him. He knew he was only trying to look out for his people. 'OK,' he replied.

'OK?'

'You can hand me over.'

Caleb had come with a host of men to take Samson by force if he'd refused, but he felt much better knowing that he'd go willingly. 'Thank you, Samson. I'll have the men wrap your arms in rope as requested by the Philistines. Then, we'll take you to them and ask they give you a fair trial. Finally, we'll

89

request that, if found guilty, they'll give you prison instead of execution—though I can't guarantee they'll honour those requests.'

Samson didn't think they would honour them, but he wasn't placing his hope in Philistine mercy. The evening after he'd set fire to the Philistine crops, ten soldiers had come for him. At first, he'd tried to explain his side of the story. But, when they told him that they'd killed his wife and that they intended to do the same to him, the alien power had come upon him once again—only this time he'd not lost his consciousness. This time he'd been fully aware of what was happening and had even felt he could direct the power flowing through him. It hadn't been him, and yet, at the same time, it had been. It was the wrath of another—yet his own anger blended with it. He was adapting.

After beating the men, he'd fled from Zorah to this cave. He'd known the Philistines would be back, and he'd wanted to keep his people safe.

Samson stood. 'Well, why are we waiting? If I'm due to dine with the Philistines, let's get a move on.' Four men came forward carrying rope and wrapped Samson's arms behind his back. They tied him tight from his wrists to his shoulders. Still, he didn't complain. These were his people, and these men were only looking out for their families.

**

Samson & the Siren

They walked for almost an hour. Caleb rode on a donkey and tried to make small talk with Samson—feeling guilty for handing him over to their oppressors.

How could I have been so blind? It was the question he'd asked himself since the drama at Serena's house. He was beginning to understand that Philistia was determined to wipe out his people—be it quickly with a soldier's sword or slowly and seductively like a piece of luscious fruit with death in the middle.

He turned to Caleb. 'Is realising your mother was right about a lot of stuff a normal part of growing up?'

Caleb smiled. 'More than you know,' he said. Samson gave a silent laugh. 'We're almost there, son. Again, I'm sorry. I wish I didn't have to. My wife and I will pray for you before bed tonight.'

'Thank you,' Samson replied, touched by the old man's sincerity. 'I'd like to request that, once you hand me over, you and the men from Judah leave quickly.'

Caleb looked at him curiously. 'Hm? Why's that?'

'Just do it. Please.'

'Well, it's your skin they'll be filleting. Not mine.'

16

SAMSON AND THE men from Judah marched over the last hill before Lehi. When Samson looked down at the valley below, he saw the Philistine host waiting—and its size of it took his breath away. 'Well, looks like a popular party,' he mumbled, half to himself, half to Caleb. The older man didn't reply.

Behind his cavalier exterior, Samson was afraid. *What if the power doesn't come?* With every step, the crowd appeared more considerable and fierce. These soldiers knew he'd killed their comrades. He wasn't expecting any mercy.

He surveyed the land around him, looking for a possible escape or sign of hope. He saw only despair. A dead and decaying donkey was lying off to the side of his path, and he could smell the stink as he approached. 'Classy,' he mumbled.

A man with a well-trimmed goatee stood at the front of the host. Several fierce young warriors stood around him with their

Samson & the Siren

swords drawn. Caleb got off his donkey and accompanied Samson on foot as the men of Judah stood at a distance.

'Here he is, General. As you requested,' Caleb said with a sober bow.

The general's face lit up—more like a performer's than a soldier's. 'Well, well, Samson! The young man that I've heard so much about lately. You've been a naughty boy it seems. Do you have anything to say for yourself?'

Samson hadn't prepared for this moment, so he opened his mouth and let his words fly. 'Your soldiers are pussies, and your women are whores.'

The soldiers surrounding the general tightened their grips on the unsheathed swords in their hands. Caleb, horrified at Samson's words, took two steps back. But the general laughed. 'Amazing. Here you are, bound and helpless as a rabbit in a trap, and yet you speak to me like this. Tell me, why shouldn't I carve your sharp tongue out of its mouth with my dagger?'

'Because then I'd have trouble eating my supper—and that would piss my mum off. Trust me. You don't wanna deal with her.'

'Yes, your mother and father. I'm aware of where they live. Perhaps, when I've finished with you, I should visit them.'

Samson hadn't yet considered that harm might come to his family. 'If you so much as touch a—' he began, but a nearby

The Oliver Anderson Trilogy

soldier sent his spear butt flying into Samson's gut, knocking the wind out of him.

'A young man who loves his parents. Charming. You know, Samson, I realise that I've been rude and forgotten to introduce myself. I am Achish, the General of National Safety.'

'Well, I gotta tell you, Achish,' Samson coughed, regaining his breath. 'I don't feel very safe at the moment. I don't like to tell another man how to do his job, but maybe if you cut me out of these ropes, put a sword in my hand, and had your men back up about a mile, I'd feel a bit safer.'

The general smiled. 'I like you, Samson.'

'Like a lion likes a gazelle?'

'Do you think I'm going to kill you?'

Samson glanced over at the dead donkey. 'I dunno, Achish. Will you?'

A look of irritation flashed across the general's face. 'First, it's "General Achish" to you. Second, that depends,' he answered, poking his finger into Samson's chest. 'I'll let you choose your destiny.'

'Really? Well, I might just go with the not killing option.'

'You haven't heard what that option entails.'

'Well, living, I'd imagine.'

Achish took a deep breath, 'As you know, we've been trying to recruit Hebrew young men to join our campaign against

94

Egypt. I wish I could say the recruitment has been a roaring success—but that would be something of an exaggeration. There are some among our leadership who think we should force Hebrew young men into military service.'

'Why don't you?'

'For two reasons. First, forced soldiers often aren't very reliable. Their hearts simply aren't in it. Secondly, although we *are* your overlords, it has been the experience of the Philistines that, if we oppress a smaller nation too hard, it backfires. Then we'd risk open war or insurrectionist fires—and we can't afford that right now.'

'Enlightening—I'll probably be up all night reflecting on how wonderful this knowledge is. But I'm still not sure what this has to do with you not killing me?'

'Instead of me killing you, I'd like you to work for me.'

Samson coughed. 'Excuse me?'

'You seemed surprised. You shouldn't be. It is perfectly reasonable. I've heard you are an exceptional fighter. What you did to those ten soldiers I sent after you was amazing. Truly, I don't know how you did it.'

'What is it you want me to do?'

'Egypt.'

'You want me to fight Egypt?'

'Well, not by yourself, of course. What I'm proposing is that you recruit twenty men that you can train and lead as captain. You will join our army on the front lines in Egypt, where we'll give you select missions. You'd be a Hebrew special forces. If you can train your men to fight like you fought my soldiers, I think your elite group would be a formidable unit. What do you say?'

'I can't say the thought of working for Philistia excites me much, Achish.'

'Why? Are you in the pay of Egypt too?'

'The pay of Egypt?'

'Yes, like your dead wife's cousin?'

Samson paused. 'Um, what are we talking about now?'

'We found the jewellery and honey pot. We know Egypt has been trying to establish a fifth column of insurgents for years now. It seems your wife's cousin and her husband Phicol were compromised.'

Samson's mind raced back to the wedding. He only vaguely remembered meeting Phicol and Marna. 'Are you sure you know what you're talking about?'

'We found evidence. Of course, they denied it. But we examined Phicol's voting record in the assembly—he consistently voted against war with Egypt,' Achish said. 'He won't be doing that anymore.'

Samson shook his head. 'Look, I know little about your politics, and, frankly, I don't give a dog's ass.'

'I don't need you to get involved in politics. Just fight for us.'

'And if I turn your offer down?'

Achish smiled. 'Then we kill you.'

In that smile, Samson saw everything poisonous about the Philistine treatment of Israel. It looked so reasonable, so classy—yet behind it all was death. Anger swelled up inside of him. He looked over his shoulder at Caleb and said, 'Now, Caleb. Now is the time to take your men away.'

Caleb didn't understand what was happening, but there was something about Samon's tone that made him uneasy enough to back off and lead his men to do the same. As he did, Samson turned to Achish, teeth clenched.

'Come on now, what's your answer?' Achish asked. 'Will you work for us?'

Samson spat on the ground. 'You can take your offer to hell. I'm going home for dinner.'

The general's smile faded. 'Oh, Samson, you disappoint me. Now, not only am I going to kill you, but I'll head back to Zorah and burn your parents and your quaint little goat farm to the ground. Maybe I'll even take your neighbours out as well. Of course, I'd rather not have to, but I'm afraid you've left me with no choice.'

97

Samson's heart began to race. His body felt the tension grow. 'Egypt has never bothered my family or me. The last time we Hebrews were in Egypt, we left them in such a bad way as to ensure they'd never mess with us again. You don't seem to have heard that story, Achish.'

'It's "General", and now you're starting to bore me.'

'Shut your fat Philistine face!' Samson yelled so loudly that he made the nearby soldiers jump. 'You come here and threaten my people. You tax us, and the sole benefit we get is that you don't attack us openly. You let us intermarry, but you do it in such a way as to ensure that we join your nation and not the other way around.'

'Guards, get the fuel!' Achish barked.

Samson continued, undeterred in his rant. 'Then you come here today and command that I kill Egyptians for you—or you'll kill me? Go. Leave our territory, and never come back.'

Achish gave a faint grin. 'Is that all?'

'No. As you go, apologise to every Hebrew home you pass for the decades of oppression you've puked over us.'

A soldier approached Achish with a leather pouch. 'Here, General.'

Achish began to open the pouch. 'I think I'll pass on that option. Frankly, I'd rather poke my eye out than apologise to your filth.'

Samson's body was full of tension as hatred at the Philistine treatment of Israel coursed through his veins. He felt a weight descend on his shoulders. He had been unsure of its source before, but now he was sure this power was from Heaven. He growled. 'Don't bother. I'll take care of that for you.'

'What?' the general asked, unsure of what he meant. 'Oh, never mind. Who wants to see this Hebrew bastard burn?' he shouted, turning to the troops standing behind him. A mighty roar rose from the host as the general turned back to Samson and smiled. 'It's my job to keep Philistia safe and, well, you're just too much of a risk.'

And, with that, several things happened all at once.

First, the general pulled back his arm to douse Samson with fuel from his leather sack. At that exact moment, however, the Heavenly force exploded inside of Samson. He tore his arms free from the ropes as if they were warm butter. As he did so, he lunged towards the general with his arm and fingers outstretched as if he was a human spear. Before the fuel could fly from the pouch, Samson buried his three middle fingers into the general's left eye socket.

The soldiers froze, the general screamed, and Samson used that moment of confusion to arm himself with the first thing that came into his mind: the jawbone of the dead donkey. In a flash, he had the large bone in his hand and plunged himself

99

into the crowd with a force and a fury that no one present had ever experienced. The host of soldiers fell apart in panic and confusion. Some began to run away. Others ran towards the fighting, and, in the chaos, many fell under the stampede of their fellow soldiers.

At the centre, Samson wielded the jawbone with unworldly efficiency, shattering skull after human skull. Blood and brains flew into the air as Philistine heads exploded. Samson was fully aware, fully conscious. He was making the decisions, but the power wasn't his. It was as if he was steering a team of stallions with every stroke he took.

The fighting went on for over half an hour—though it felt much longer. When it was all done, Samson was on his knees, in the middle of a sea of bodies. Fled, trampled, or killed with the jawbone of an ass, they were no more. He was alone. His hand had melded to the bone, and the blood, skin, and organs of his enemies covered his body.

Though Samson had been in control, he was shocked at what had just occurred. He'd never witnessed such a slaughter nor even heard of one. He trembled under the terror of what had happened—under the knowledge of what he was capable of.

He was wounded. More than one blade had touched his skin, but none had cut too deeply. Still, he bled. But it wasn't

Samson & the Siren

his cuts that hurt the most. It was his thirst. He may have had the power of Heavenly wrath, but his body was still human, and the fighting had dehydrated him to the point of death.

Samson looked up to the sky and lifted his bloody and aching arms. 'Yahweh, God of Heaven. It was you who pulled off this great deliverance through me. But what does it matter if I die of thirst and the Philistines find my body?' he cried as he fell, face forward.

He lay still, life oozing out of him. But then, there was a tremble. The earth ripped open, and a spring of water shot into the air. It fell to the ground and flowed straight to Samson. Slowly, he leaned his head to the side and lapped up the water like an injured dog.

How long he lay like that, he couldn't tell. But his strength slowly returned as he drank. As it did, the thought of all that had transpired flashed through his mind. Suddenly, as he lay there in pain, his sense of calling became clear. It's what his parents had always told him, but he had never wanted to hear.

So, it's for real. Samson knew with certainty that he was to lead Israel—to ensure they had freedom and justice.

But not tonight. For tonight, Samson would hobble home, lick his wounds, and eat his dinner.

The Oliver Anderson Trilogy

17

ELISE SMILED. 'YOUR grandpa's story reminds me of the accounts my family told me.'

Oliver looked at his girlfriend, sitting next to him in William's hospital room. 'How so?'

'After the war, when the Communists came to power, some Christians were hopeful that the church could exist happily within the new system. After all, they used positive-sounding words like "equality" and "justice". Weren't Christians supposed to want these things too? Some tried to make friends and build bridges with the new government. But, in the end, the Communist rules and regulations crushed us—we had to go underground for decades.'

'How am I your boyfriend, and don't know this?'

'These are my parents' stories. Not mine. I was born after the system collapsed and Czechoslovakia split in two.'

Samson & the Siren

'And you were born in the Czech side, right?'

Elise winked. 'I'm glad you know that much.'

William laughed. 'Welcome to life with a woman, Oliver. I'd like to tell ye one day you'll figure it all out, but that'd be less than honest.'

'Thanks,' Oliver said. 'Any more nuggets of wisdom there, Yoda?'

'By listening to the woman, learn you will.'

'Your grandpa's a smart man,' Elise said.

Oliver threw his hands up. 'OK, before you two gang up on me, I'd like to get back to the subject. Grandpa, what do you know about what the church in Eastern Europe suffered?'

'It was bad.'

'Um, thanks?'

'It was your question, knucklehead.'

'I'll rephrase. How do Christians, like those in Eastern Europe, know when to work with the government and when to resist?'

'Ah, gotcha. Well, it's not an easy question. Christians have had a back and forth relationship with civil governments for 2,000 years now. It doesn't always work well. Christians, by definition, are loyal to Christ as their King. As for the civil government, Jesus told his followers, "Give unto Caesar what is Caesar's and give unto God what is God's." The difficulty is that not all Christians agree about what belongs to Caesar—while Caesar tends to have an ever-growing opinion about what belongs to him. That's why there's disagreement about when to dissent and when to submit.'

'It looks like Samson figured it out.'

'Not exactly. God called Samson to lead Israel out from under Philistine oppression. But, instead of obeying that call, he tried to have a cosy relationship with his overlords and thus avoid conflict. So it wasn't moral conviction that gave birth to his resistance—it was a personal offence.'

'So he began fighting the right battles, but for the wrong reasons?'

'Something like that, laddie.'

'It's not always clear,' Elise interjected, 'when to battle for what you believe in and when to quietly and submissively go with the flow.'

'I'm glad we don't have to face what your parents and grandparents faced back East.'

'Not yet,' Elise said.

'That sounds pessimistic.'

'You should talk to my parents about this, Oliver. They see this country moving in a dangerous direction—they'd say it's increasingly similar to what they grew up with.'

Samson & the Siren

Oliver's eyebrows jumped. 'Really? They think we're about to have a communist takeover?'

'Not exactly. But they'll both tell you that Britain, as with much of the West, is not as free as when we moved here.'

'Really?'

'Yes, it's true. People are afraid to share political opinions openly,' Elise said. 'They whisper them when they're in a crowded room. Surely you've heard stories of people losing their job because of some political comment they put on social media.'

'But that's nothing like what your family suffered back in Eastern Europe.'

'No. Not yet, anyway. For now, it's softer and more subtle.'

'The Soviet leaders built the USSR on the notion that everyone in society should conform to an ideology,' William added. 'This policin' of people's minds is still is a harsh reality in China, and it's becoming more popular here in the West. It's a "pink" totalitarianism. Forced control, but with a smile.'

Oliver shook his head. 'I dunno guys. I find it hard to compare Britain with Communist China or the Soviets.'

'What about what's going on right now back in London? You know, with the school?' Elise asked.

'With your film?'

'Yes, and MAGBT.'

The Oliver Anderson Trilogy

Oliver mused for a moment. 'OK, I guess MAGBT does involve a bit of mind policing.'

'What's this?' William asked.

'Have you heard of MAGBT, grandpa?'

'Certainly. It's a group that wields a lot of influence in both government and corporations.'

'The MAGBT ideology is part of our school's new value statement. You see, they chose Elise's script several months back to be this year's production piece. She directed it, and the school will release it in a couple of weeks. But a certain teacher is pointing out that her film doesn't do anything for the MAGBT cause and is pressuring Elise to make small changes to it.'

'But I don't know if I should,' Elise said, lowering her shoulders. 'They're trying to make me change it to advance ideas I don't embrace. I'm not sure what to do. Am I just being stubborn?'

'I don't think so,' Oliver said. 'It's your film, not theirs. They signed up to MAGBT, not you.'

'From the moment I got the first email from this teacher, I began to think of my grandparents—how they had such moral strength and clarity. I'm not sure I have what they did—or perhaps I'm unsure if compromising with MAGBT is all that

Samson & the Siren

bad. Either way, I still haven't made up my mind how to respond. It has me stressed.'

'I'm here for you, baby,' Oliver said, placing his hand on her knee. 'Anything I can do?'

'End all oppression and make the world free?'

'No problem. Would you like a side dish of endless happiness for everyone with that?'

Elise laughed and then placed her hand on his. 'Just that you offer is a big help,' she said and kissed him.

'Anytime,' Oliver said with a grin. Then he turned to his grandpa. 'It's tough to have to pretend you believe in a certain ideology—or else have your education or job at risk.'

'May I ask,' William began, 'What would happen if ye didn't make the changes? Would they refuse to release your film?'

'They might threaten to do that,' Elise said, 'But, as the release is only a couple of weeks away, I think it would be a bluff. Still, if I'm not cooperative, it can hurt me in other ways later on. It's the administration that awards grades and recognition. They help students find jobs after they've finished.'

'So if ye don't comply, it's a mark on your record that might not go away. That it?'

'Yes.'

'Hm. A hard situation to be in, but nothing new for believers.'

The Oliver Anderson Trilogy

Oliver took Elise's hand. 'I'm sorry you have to go through this. But, if you choose to go against the school administration, I'm sure many students will support you.'

'Thank you. But I'm not sure they will. MAGBT ideas aren't just popular with corporations. They're trendy in the arts community and among young adults too.'

Oliver knew she was right. 'Yeah, I suppose. It's everywhere. What would you do, grandpa?'

'Don't worry about what I'd do. Elise needs to follow her own conscience on this. Pray. Live with integrity. Be who you are and live by the truth.'

Elise smiled. 'Thank you, grandpa. I want to do what's right. Still, I'm not naturally a rule-breaker. I love my grandparents and their stories, but I don't think I could ever go against authority figures as they did.'

'Well, I'm sure you'll do better than Samson did.'

'Ha! Thanks,' she said. 'Speaking of him, I've had enough of unloading my MAGBT problems on you boys,' Elise said, clapping her hands together. 'Please tell me more of the story. I want to get my mind off school stresses.'

'Well, if that's what'd you like, I'm happy to continue.'

'Thanks.'

William cleared his throat and continued. 'Some time passed after the incident with the foxes and Serena's murder. Samson

Samson & the Siren

began to lead his people and help build up small militias. He led Israel for several years and avoided capture by the Philistine authorities, particularly General Achish—who pursued him with his remaining eye.

18

ISRAEL

ELEVEN YEARS LATER

'YOU'LL HAVE ONE-third of the harvest. Your brother will have two-thirds.'

Two men stood in front of Samson. One smiled, the other protested. 'But why should he get twice as much?'

Samson was annoyed. It had been a long day of judging cases—a part of his role that he didn't enjoy. But Samson was a leader-judge and, as such, he needed to protect his people both from themselves and outsiders alike.

'Look, Isaac,' Samson growled. 'I won't explain this again. You two might share the land, but the evidence demonstrated that your brother worked those fields this year while you did not. He, therefore, gets the double-portion.'

'Does it count for nothing that I'm the oldest?'

'Go!' Samson roared, and the older brother scurried off. The younger bowed and departed, thankful that Samson had rendered justice for him.

Samson got off his seat and headed back to the goats. As the only child, he'd inherited everything when his parents passed away, first his mother and then, two years later, his father. Though he was based at the farm, he spent much of his time travelling through the region—a lifestyle that made it difficult for his enemies to predict where he might be at any given time. Meanwhile, the daily running of the farm fell to Malachi and the servants who still managed to profit from his parents' business. Meanwhile, whether at the farm or elsewhere, Samson gave himself to judging, defending, and equipping the people of Israel in the face of Philistine oppression.

'Malachi, how's the shearing?'

'Very well, sir,' the elder servant replied. 'We managed seventy-five today.'

'Seventy-five goats? Is that a record?'

'The best under your father was sixty-eight. Now we only have fifty more to shave tomorrow.'

Samson rubbed his hand over his long hair. 'Shaving? I wouldn't know much about that.'

Malachi laughed. 'No, and I suppose you never will,' he said. 'Do you still intend to leave first thing in the morning?'

'No, I've changed my mind. I'll head out tonight and make camp in the hills. I don't want to waste time.'

'Tonight? Shall I have someone load the donkey with supplies?'

'No, thank you. I want to travel light. Have someone put a wineskin, bread, and some meat in a sack for me—just enough for a late-night meal. The rest I'll buy as I travel."

'As you wish, sir.'

'In the meantime, I'll head inside and trim my beard—don't wanna stick out too much.'

'A wise move, sir. Do you still intend to be gone for ten days?'

'About ten. Maybe two weeks. It depends on how fast I travel, what I discover, and how fat I get eating all that Philistine food.'

Malachi smiled. 'And you're sure you don't want to go with anyone?'

'Nah, I'll do this one solo.'

'You mean "alone", sir?'

Samson paused. He knew his servant was trying to help him. 'To travel with a group would only draw attention.'

'Maybe just one friend? Moses said it wasn't good for man to be alone,' Malachi said in a humble yet fatherly way.

Samson & the Siren

'A friend? Like who? Look, if I'm gonna get the information we need, I gotta stay incognito, right?'

'Yes, sir. I'll prepare your sack. But, please, come back safe.'

Samson winked. 'Hey, it's me.'

***

Samson shaved, dressed in the Philistine fashion, and headed out. He preferred travelling to settling disputes between his countrymen. He felt that, by spying out the changing landscape of Philistia, he was doing something that made a difference and would help him strengthen Israeli defences.

Not that he wouldn't enjoy the journey. He enjoyed walking along the sea from Ashdod to Askelon to Gaza. He enjoyed watching the ships come in and out of the harbours—something that, as an inland people, one never saw among the Hebrews. The truth was, even after a decade of open hostility to Philistine dominance, he still found aspects of their culture intriguing. Though he'd never admit it to those he led, he still enjoyed Philistine art, music, and food.

And the women. He still had a robust appetite for Philistine women. One part of the trip that he hadn't discussed with Malachi was the brothels he'd be staying at in every Philistine town—the real reason he preferred travelling alone. For Samson, Philistine prostitutes were an ideal solution: they could satisfy his appetites without breaking his heart as Serena once

113

had. Moreover, he could enjoy them without dirtying either his reputation or any of the Hebrew women he was called to protect.

It did have a tragic drawback, however, and Samson was only now becoming aware of it. Samson had become a profoundly lonely man—and his emptiness would soon catch up with him.

19

PHILISTIA

DELILAH UNLOCKED THE door to her apartment, which sat above a fabric shop off a noisy street near the middle of Gath. She kicked off her sandals and brought her sack of bread, cinnamon sticks, and olive oil into the kitchen.

The apartment was more than most twenty-year-old, unmarried women could afford: tiled, spacious, and well decorated in a young, Aegean fashion. It had a large balcony on its east side, facing the mountains, which would send a cool breeze Delilah's way morning and evening. The kitchen and dining area were small—there was rarely more than two people in at any one time—and it had two bedrooms. The smaller bedroom was for Goliath whenever he got leave from fighting. The larger bedroom was hers. That's where she rested.

And where she worked.

It was late morning, and Delilah hadn't eaten yet. She laid her sack on the counter and pulled out the fresh bread while leaving the bottle of oil and cinnamon. Those items Delilah would use later with her client. She looked over at the small idol, squatting at the end of the counter. 'Goddess, protect my brother today. Keep him alive,' she whispered—as was her daily habit. She bent down and took out a piece of cheese wrapped in linen from a box below the counter, grabbed a knife, and proceeded to slice.

That's when she heard the whistle.

Instinctively, her hand tightened on the knife handle. She knew the acoustics of her apartment. She was used to sounds drifting up out of the city streets and through her window. That whistle, however, was not from outside.

She spun around with the knife firmly in her right hand, but no one was there. She stepped into the next room and saw no one. Then she heard the whistle again. It was coming from down the hallway. She tip-toed slowly past her brother's room and peeked inside: no one there. She took a few more steps and arrived at the thin curtain that separated her bedroom from the hallway. She inched it away from the doorpost and peeked in.

A man was sitting on her bed with his back towards her, facing the window. She knew from the man's build and the grey specks in his hair that it wasn't her brother.

Samson & the Siren

She stretched out the knife in front of her and inched her way towards the intruder. Her mind raced as she considered what to do once she got within striking distance. It crossed her mind that he might not be a thief—perhaps he was a confused, would-be client. She took note of his clothes. They looked official. Was she in trouble of some kind?

Once she got close enough to stab, the man spoke. 'Hello, Delilah,' he said in a calm voice and turned to face her. 'Please forgive the intrusion. You have a lovely view from this window. Do your clients ever say so?' Delilah stepped backwards and dropped the knife. It clattered on the tile floor as the man stood and walked towards her.

It was him.

His well-trimmed goatee, general's uniform, sly smile and large, white teeth were as she'd remembered. Only two things were different: the touch of grey in his hair and a patch over his left eye.

Over the last five years, Delilah had cultivated the skill of appearing one way to men while feeling very different on the inside. She knew how to hide her emotions and bury her soul. Usually, she had time to prepare herself, time to step into her role as a performer. But caught unexpected—and by this man of all people—there was no hiding. She continued backing into

The Oliver Anderson Trilogy

the hall while the general calmly walked after her. Her eyes darted for an escape. Nothing. 'G-get away from me!'

'Come now. You've already dropped your knife. You're not going to hurt me, and I haven't come to hurt you.' Her body trembled at the sound of his voice. She knew it only too well. She'd only ever heard it once before—eleven years previous— but she hadn't forgotten its haunting quality. She'd heard it over and over again in her nightmares. 'Since you're leading me down the hallway, why don't we sit in your dining area. There are pillows for two where we can have a much-needed conversation.'

'I have a client,' she spat out. 'He'll be here soon.'

'Oh? Do you mean the merchant from Ashkelon?' he asked, stroking his beard, 'I was under the impression he had business before members of the Assembly until the fifth hour. That gives us plenty of time.'

'H-how do you know—?' she began to ask, sweat coming down her face.

'Oh, I think you know how I know,' he said. 'Ah, yes. I can see in your eyes that you remember me.'

Of course, she did. How could she ever forget? He was the man who'd taken her parents away—and with her parents, everything else, including her virginity.

Samson & the Siren

20

DELILAH SHIVERED AS she sat on the pillow, hands clasped together. The general sat across from her, holding a cup of wine. Delilah's cup was on the tray in front of her and, though it was untouched, she focused her gaze on it to avoid looking at her unwanted guest.

'You're a beautiful but quiet hostess. Perhaps you could ask me, as your guest, how I am. Or, if you want to jump straight to business, you could ask me what I'm doing here.'

Delilah knew she had to pull herself together. She possessed the ability to put on whatever face her company most desired but seeing this monster from her past made her feel like a little child again. She took a deep breath and lifted her eyes. *What does he want?* she wondered. 'I'm a free subject of Philistia. I run my own business and choose my clients as I see fit.'

The general's laugh bordered on the theatrical. 'No, no, no. You don't understand, my dear.'

What mask shall I wear? she wondered. The general both terrified and infuriated her—but she didn't want him to see those feelings any more than he already had. For a moment, she thought about being a strong and bold woman who'd throw him out. But then she saw the dagger by his side. *No,* she thought, *that might backfire. Go with coy and seductive.* Not something she'd enjoy, but given the circumstances, she knew it would be her best shot at survival.

He finished his chuckle and looked into her eyes. 'No, I'm afraid I didn't come here to mount you.'

Then why are you here, pervert? 'To what do I owe the honour of my lord's visit?' she asked with a smile.

'I didn't come for *that* but,' he said, looking her body up and down, 'perhaps later. I'm more than happy to ravish you again. Eleven years is a long time, and your body has filled out nicely.'

Delilah maintained her smile. Her eyes shot back to his dagger. 'Can I pour you some more wine, sir?'

'Yes, please,' he said. 'Delilah, I've come with a proposition for you.'

All men come to me with a proposition, you piece of garbage. 'Oh? And what might that be?'

'We have an issue of national safety that needs addressing.'

Samson & the Siren

Delilah squinted and turned her head to the side. 'Safety?' she asked, surprised.

'Yes. I'm the general of National Safety. It's a role that might change soon—if we bring our men back from Egypt.'

Delilah thought of her brother. 'Bring them back?'

'Our campaign in the South has lasted over fifteen years. We've little to show for it even though we've lost troops by the thousands. There's a growing political will to redeploy our troops along our Eastern border instead.'

'Yes, they'd be safer back here.' Her tone betrayed her excitement.

'Yes, along our border with the Hebrews.'

Delilah was suspicious of any good news that proceeded from his mouth. 'Do you go around to all the sisters of soldiers to deliver this good news?'

'I deal with conflicts on the borderlands,' he replied, not answering her question. 'If our troops withdraw from Egypt, they'll reengage in open war with the Hebrews. I'd like to deal with a major problem we have there before I hand this role over to anyone else.'

Like I care, scumbag. 'You must be a very competent man for the Philistine Lords to entrust you with that much authority.'

121

Achish smiled. 'They've seen fit to put the nation's internal safety under my care for over a decade.'

National Safety, what kind of a title is that? Do you go around making sure kids don't run around near open fires? 'Amazing. I don't know how you get it all done,' she said with an admiring smile.

Her words were drawing him in. 'Yes, it is a lot of work—so many risks and so many people to keep safe. This is why I seek your services.'

Delilah was curious. 'How can a little gal like me be of any service to a mighty general like you?'

'Don't sell yourself short. I hear you're good at what you do.'

If he thinks this visit will involve a blowjob, then, I swear, whatever he puts in my mouth won't come out in one piece. 'How can I please you, my lord?'

'Have you heard of the Hebrew they call "Samson"?'

Huh? 'Yes, all Philistia has heard of that troublemaker.'

'He's a demon,' Achish spat. 'He's given us trouble for nearly a decade.'

'Are you not able to find him?'

'We know where his business is based, though he moves about a lot all through the Sorek and beyond.'

'Can't you send in the army?'

Samson & the Siren

'No. You see, we're not officially at war and my powers to hunt that terrorist are limited. I can't send in the whole army, and my attempts at traping him or sending in small units have been less than successful.'

So this Hebrew is showing you up. 'It's all very fascinating, but I still don't see how I can help.'

'It's not just the militias he raises up—irritating though they are. It's his strength in battle. He has the powers of hell flowing through him. I've seen him battle afar and up close.'

And is he the one who took your eye? 'Up close, you say? I hope that demon didn't do you any harm,' she said as she scooted herself closer. The dagger was almost within grabbing distance.

Achish took a deep breath. 'Never mind what he's done to me. It's a matter of professional pride that I remove this thorn before I hand responsibility for the region over to the next general. He will, in all probability, lead a large scale invasion into Israel, and I don't want it said that he first has to clean up a mess that I couldn't take care of myself.'

Delilah still didn't see what any of this had to do with her. 'If you can't send in the army, and small units are unsuccessful, how do you plan on getting rid of him?'

'He has a weakness.'

'Oh?'

'Yes, Philistine women.'

Delilah's mouth opened. She thought she could see where this was going. 'Are you asking me to sleep with the enemy, General?'

'It's more than sex. A common whore could scratch that itch. We've reason to believe he's emotionally vulnerable.'

'How could you know such a thing?'

'According to our spies, he has no wife or children. Servants and fighting men look up to him, but he has no real companions. He has followers, not friends. In addition, Samson was in Gaza three weeks ago. He was undercover and staying, as is his habit, at one of the city's brothels. The local soldiers tried to capture him, but he overpowered them and broke the city gates in the process.'

Another failure on your part, rat. 'That was brave of your soldiers to try and stop him.'

'We interrogated the last whore he rented. He only spent a short time screwing her—but spent hours talking with her afterwards. He asked about her life and opened up about his. He even told her about the death of his parents and recounted childhood memories.'

So you're a crazed man hunting a sad man. 'Sounds like this devil is less interested in a prostitute and more in a long-term mistress—or a wife.'

124

'Yes, I imagine you know the type: horny bodies *and* lonely hearts. We want you to use that against him.'

'What, exactly, are you asking me to do?' Delilah asked.

'Get close. Earn Samon's trust.'

Delilah still couldn't see why the general was asking her to do this. 'How will that help you defeat him?'

'He doesn't fight with his own strength—he has the power of a hundred devils! We need to understand how it works so we can neutralise it.'

Delilah couldn't hold back a cough of disbelief. 'Build a relationship with a Hebrew warrior in hopes of uncovering a secret? I may be a whore, but I've never learned espionage.'

Achish smiled. 'Oh, I think you'd do fine.'

'No. It's too dangerous. What if this Samson attacks me?'

'We'll give you strong servants that are soldiers in disguise. Even the female ones we give you for your intimate affairs will be capable of wielding a blade. You'll have the perfect cover. He'll have no reason to suspect you.'

She glanced at his dagger and began to rock her body into position. 'I don't know, General. I feel you've got the wrong girl. I'm not that brave.'

'I can give you three reasons why you're the right choice,' he said.

This should be amusing. 'I'm listening.'

The Oliver Anderson Trilogy

'First, you're no ordinary whore. Yes, you make a living with your tits, but you don't live in a brothel. Your beauty and ability to please men have brought you more wealth than most girls in your line of work. Second, you're smart. You came from high breeding. That's rare among whores—and probably why you're successful at nabbing wealthy men. You're cultured. This man is also well off. This job requires someone with sharp brains as well as a nice rack.'

'I see,' Delilah said. 'What's the third?'

Achish's smile turned dark. 'Third, not only are you a good whore, but you're also a good liar.'

She pretended to pout. 'Why would you think I'm a liar?'

'First, you've convinced five wealthy assemblymen that you're their exclusive mistress. Few whores could pull that off for very long. Second, it's what you're doing right now.'

Uh-oh. 'Right now?'

'Have you calculated it yet? Are you waiting for the moment I turn my right eye to take the dagger you keep glancing at?'

Delilah's blood ran cold. 'Y-you doubt my admiration for you, Achish?'

He roared with laughter. 'My dear, you're good. But I've spent my whole life dealing with liars. Save your batting eyelashes for now—we need to talk business.'

126

Delilah took a deep breath and shuffled back. She didn't like anyone knowing how she felt or what she thought. Her hand grabbed the glass of wine in front of her and chugged it all in one go. 'Look,' she said, wiping her mouth. 'I don't need to hear anymore. No! The gods didn't create enough curses for me to respond adequately to your putrid proposal.'

Achish grinned. 'Charming. But you'll agree when you hear what I offer.'

'Go to hell,' she said as she stood. 'Get out of my home. I'm a free citizen of Philistia, and I refuse your—'

'First, the Philistine lords have agreed to pay you in silver five years of your annual salary for this mission—which should only take a few months at most.'

Delilah's eyes popped wide. That *was* a lot of money. At least the general wasn't trying to force her to do this unpaid. She was well off as an independent whore with high-end connections— but this type of money was on a whole new level.

Then she remembered that this was the man who'd murdered her parents. Loathing pumped through her veins once again. 'I don't want your money. Screw the Hebrew yourself, you big pussy. Now get ou—'

'Second,' Achish continued, unphased by her scorn, 'I'll give you back your childhood home for the whole of the mission.

That is where you will live—and where you will be taken care of by the servants we provide.'

Delilah had longed for that home ever since she and her brother had lost it as children. She dreamed that one day she'd have enough money to repurchase those lands. *How could he know what I'm saving for?* 'Explain,' she said with her arms crossed.

'You'd move up North. It'll be part of your cover. Samson's activities are based there in the Sorek Valley, where his servants run a large goat farm. You'd pose as a wealthy heiress who's new to the area and learning how to care for the estate.'

Delilah paused. It was a good offer. But then her conscience rebuked her for even considering a deal with this man. 'I shouldn't have to pretend those lands are mine. I really should be a wealthy heiress to those lands—but you took my inheritance from my brother and me along with my parents. Get out of my house, now! If the gods have predestined it, I'll reclaim my home one day without the help of a monster like you!'

'OK. You're driving a hard bargain,' the general remarked, noting her stubbornness. 'What about Goliath?'

Hearing her brother's name from his lips was like a splash of cold water. 'Don't you ever mention him!'

Samson & the Siren

'What would you do for your brother? Hm? Anything, from what I gather.'

'What is that supposed to mean?'

'Don't you know I can make or break him?' the general asked, standing up. 'If you agree, I'll ensure your brother gets brought back from Egypt immediately—regardless of whether there's a troop withdrawal or not. Moreover, I'll give him a safe job—one as well paying as any eighteen-year-old soldier could desire. An assistant warden, perhaps?'

There was no amount of wealth Achish could've offered her that would've made Delilah work with him. But there was also nothing she wouldn't do for Goliath. 'You'd do that for him if I attempt this for you? I can't promise success.'

'I understand. If you agree, I'll put your brother's transfer in motion immediately.'

She bit her lip. She hated that this man had something valuable to her. 'If I accept, it's not for the money, the nation, or you—it'll be for my brother.'

Achish bowed. 'Whatever helps you sleep at night, my dear,' he said with a grin and turned to the door. 'But I need your answer by tomorrow at the latest.'

She nodded. 'You'll have it.'

The Oliver Anderson Trilogy

21

'SO ACHISH IS sending Delilah to seduce Samson. Is that it?' Oliver asked.

Elise chuckled. 'Are men really always thinking about one thing?'

'Aye. We might say that the weaker sex is the stronger sex because of the stronger sex's weakness for the weaker sex,' Grandpa William said with a shrug of his shoulders. 'And it's a weakness General Achish will use against Samson. Sexual immorality is the drug most tyrants give to the masses to soften their love of liberty.'

'How do you mean, grandpa?'

'When the Communists took over Russia, they promised the masses they'd do away with the "strict" sexual morals of the Orthodox Church. When Moab wanted to defeat Israel in the wilderness, they sent the pretty lassies to seduce the soldiers.

And, in our generation, we've bathed everyone in porn. It's numbed us so much that we're apathetic about liberty and no longer care if it's Big Tech or Big Government monitorin' us online. If ye surrender to inner, sensual tyrants, it'll weaken yer resolve to resist outer, civil tyrants. True freedom begins in yer spirit then works its way outward into society. The Christian Gospel works to liberate men and women from sin. It's only downstream that civil freedoms begin to grow.'

'Excuse me, boys.' Elise said, standing up. 'I need to find a toilet.'

'I think we passed one near reception on the way in,' Oliver said.

'Thanks. I'll be back in a minute.'

When the door shut, William turned to his grandson and said, 'She's fantastic! Hurry up and marry her before she realises yer not much of a catch.'

'Gee, thanks for the advice.'

'Anytime, lad. Look, there are fewer and fewer women out there who are truly lovely in the classical, feminine sense. I've been watchin' how she interacts with ye since ye arrived, and she's one of 'em. She appreciates ye protectin' her and isn't trying to compete with you. That's gold!'

'Alright, grandpa, but, for now, we just want to graduate without causing too much of a fuss on campus. What do you

The Oliver Anderson Trilogy

think: should she fight the school over the MAGBT issue?'

'Knowing when to submit and when to resist is not always easy for people to discern. Christians aren't against the government or civic leaders. But when a Christian believes a law is unjust, their first loyalty is always to Christ. He's our ultimate King—not a prime minister, president, or school administration. Knox, the great Scottish reformer, said, "Resistance to tyranny is obedience to God".'

'So she should resist?'

'She needs to follow the Scriptures and her conscience before God. Ye might live that out differently than I would, but that's fine. We're each ultimately accountable to Christ alone.'

Oliver smiled. 'So you're not saying we should do a hunger strike then?'

'Ha! Who knows? Pray first, then do what ye believe is right. And, if other Christians tell you they would've done it differently, then don't worry. It won't be the first time Christians have disagreed on how to respond to unjust authority.'

'Like when?'

'How familiar are ye with the Jim Crow Laws that existed in the American South?'

'The ones Martin Luther King Jr marched against?'

'Yep.'

Samson & the Siren

'We covered that in history class.'

'Well, the churches were caught up in the middle of all this social unrest. But they disagreed with each other on how to respond to the situation.'

'I don't see what's so confusing about *that* situation. It was pretty clear: the churches should've all been marching with King.'

'Moral hindsight is 20/20. It's easy to look back at a past generation and say how they shoulda behaved. But, livin' in the middle of a situation makes ye see shades of moral grey.'

'How was segregation unclear morally?'

'Many church leaders knew racial segregation was wrong, but they chose not to fight it.'

'Why?'

'For some, it was their understanding of passages in the New Testament like Romans 13. They saw segregation as the law and thought the Christian duty was to submit to civil laws—even if they weren't good ones. Others didn't believe it was the job of a pastor to speak about socio-political issues. They thought they should preach salvation with no reference to the morality of the problems outside the church.'

'Was it *really* that complicated for them?'

'For some ministers, it felt complicated,' William said. 'Others knew segregation was wrong but didn't bring the racial issue up because they didn't want to divide the church or see people leave. It's difficult when close friends and family disagree on charged issues.'

'But how could any Christian go along with Jim Crow laws? Surely the church should've been united in fighting them.'

'Sadly, that wasn't the case. Sure, ye had some people who were openly racist. But, for most, Christians had reasons and justifications that sounded respectable.'

Oliver crossed his arms and raised an eyebrow. 'Such as?'

'In Southern cities, disease and viral infections were more common in black neighbourhoods than in the white ones. Many church-goin' whites claimed to have no animosity towards blacks, but they didn't want to mix for health and safety reasons. So if a black family showed up at their white church and put their black children in Sunday school, some parents would object that their kids were at medical risk.'

'So they were just trying to "stay safe"—was that the excuse?'

'Yep. Those Christians claimed to be followin' the science of the day. But, ye see, the devil loves to separate and isolate people. If he can use ethical or educated sounding reasons for doin' it, he will. Jim Crow laws weren't the first or the last time governments passed laws to keep people apart under the banner of fancy soundin' reasons.'

'I appreciate that these issues can be complicated,' Oliver

said. 'But I'm not sure how to support Elise in her current struggle with the school administration and this MAGBT mess. I want her to decide for herself what God would have her do and not to pressure her. But, when I think ahead—when I think of how I might one day explain all this to our grandkids—I hope we can tell them we didn't compromise: that we didn't bend the knee to bullies or violate our conscience.'

'Spoken like a true Anderson,' Grandpa William said.

The door opened, and Elise entered the room. 'Hey fellas, what did I miss?'

Oliver smiled. 'Grandpa was just giving me a history lesson.'

'You didn't say any more about Samson, did you?'

William smiled. 'Of course not, my dear.'

'Good,' Elise said.

'Help an old man, dear, where were we exactly?'

'The general had just hired Delilah to spy for him.'

'She's sharp, lad. Hold onto her,' William said. 'Yes, General Achish gave Delilah her old childhood home and pulled Delilah's brother off the front lines. But Achish planned on using her brother as more than a simple payment.'

The Oliver Anderson Trilogy

22

THE WARDEN OF Ekron prison looked up at the guest sitting across from him: the General of National Safety was visiting. He could, of course, be checking on one of the political prisoners that Ekron kept—though they had precious few of those compared to the much larger prison in Gath. Instead, most of their prisoners were common thieves or vandals.

He suspected, however, that it might have something to do with the new assistant the general had commanded him to take on. It had been an unusual order, and he was still trying to figure out why the military had sent the otherwise strong and healthy young man his way. Typically, he'd only ever get the semi-injured or elderly type to help him with the management and administration of the prison. Whatever the reason, a visit from the general always ignited a degree of apprehension. The warden had spent fifteen years as a soldier on the front lines and

Samson & the Siren

the last ten managing this prison. He'd seen plenty of nasty business—and even disposed of some himself.

But it was the general's particular brand of ruthless cruelty that bothered him. It was so unpredictable. Though the warden was a faithful son of Philistia, he was never sure what fault the general might find in how he ran his prison—or what punishment the general would give him as a consequence.

'Greetings, General Achish. It's been a while since your last visit. We're honoured by your presence and hope the running of this prison meets your approval.'

'Thank you, warden. You continue to do a fine job. Your prisoners are as miserable as they are trapped. Well done.'

'We're honoured that our humble prison meets with your approval. To what do we owe the pleasure of your visit? An inspection?'

Achish smiled. 'Ah, that's what I've always liked about you, warden. You're observant! You know when something is afoot, and I imagine that's why there's been precious few escapes from your prison over the years.'

'I try to pay attention, General. How can I best serve you today?'

'Straight to business, eh? That's another thing I like about you—and it's why I sent you a new assistant. How's he working out so far?'

The Oliver Anderson Trilogy

'He's been responsible enough. Willing to work hard. He's friendly. I'm not used to sharing duties with one so young, but he seems up for the job.'

'I need you to keep a special eye on him for me.'

'I assumed he must be of importance since you transferred him here from the front lines. Is he a relative of yours, General?'

'No, but he is of some importance to me—though he doesn't know it. I need him to be observed and full reports given to me once a month of his activities—particularly if you notice anything suspicious. All of this is confidential. Don't let him know you're observing him, understand?'

The warden understood that the general was asking him to spy. This assignment wasn't an activity that was part of his job description or something he would enjoy doing. 'I'll do as commanded, general. But might I ask what I should be looking for? Does he have questionable connections? Did he dishonour Philistia while in battle?'

'He has, shall we say, a peculiar family background for a soldier. But I'd rather not go into all that. Just report anything that's unusual—especially any behaviour that's unbecoming of a soldier of Philistia.'

The warden had only known Goliath for a few weeks, but he was a likeable lad. Tinkering around in someone's life until he found some fault was not a task he relished. 'You want dirt on

Samson & the Siren

him,' the warden said, more bluntly than he had intended to.

Achish smiled. 'I wouldn't have worded it like that, dear warden. But it seems you understand. Send me monthly reports on him. Will that be a problem?'

'Not at all, General. You'll receive reports each month highlighting any questionable activity,' the warden said dutifully. 'Hopefully, these reports will be short.'

'Yes… hopefully.'

The Oliver Anderson Trilogy

23

'AND YOU'RE SURE this isn't another trap?' Samson asked his silver-haired servant as he walked along the river with a goat over his shoulders.

'I've had two teams of scouts check it out. It looks like a legitimate client. I wouldn't go with you if I thought otherwise.' Malachi said.

Samson could never be too sure. In the last five years, his goat business had lost thirteen Philistine buyers and only gained one. Even with him officially 'retiring' and Malachi running the business, rumours that Samson was somehow associated with the company caused many Philistine clients to buy their goat elsewhere—even if it meant paying more.

Twice, the sudden appearance of a new Philistine client had been a trap by assassins. This potential Philistine client wanted to meet Samson in person—and that made him suspicious. Yet,

Samson & the Siren

Malachi was his eldest and most trusted servant. 'I trust you, Malachi,' Samson said. 'Still, you'll forgive me for bringing my sword.'

'It's always wise to err on the side of caution, sir.'

'So, who are they exactly? What have our spies discovered?'

'It's a woman who commands the house,' Malachi responded. 'She's moved in with twelve servants and plans to get the vineyards and olive press up and running again.'

'Is she the widow of some Philistine lord or rich merchant?'

'I don't think so. The young men reported that the woman was quite young. Twenty perhaps.'

'Twenty and not married? The Philistines are a strange lot. If she's unmarried at twenty, she must be a real camel's arse.'

'Perhaps, sir. But looks hardly matters in securing a good business deal.'

'Hopefully, Miss Camel is inexperienced enough not to know the going rate of fresh goat meat.'

'I doubt we'll be speaking with her directly, sir. I imagine she'll have a more experienced servant who'll examine what we've brought and make a deal with us.'

Samson nodded. 'Of course. Do you know why she's choosing to buy from us?'

'She's probably heard we provide the best goats anywhere in the Sorek region,' Malachi said.

141

Samson smiled. 'And *not* heard that our business funds a Hebrew militia.'

'No. Hopefully, she won't learn about that anytime soon.'

The men stopped for a short water break and then continued their two-hour journey West to the new client's house. He had passed this estate before but had never given it a close look. No one from here had either been a potential client or posed a military threat.

As they walked through the vineyards and towards the house, Samson couldn't help but be impressed. He counted three separate wine vats and saw an olive orchard with two large presses. Closer to the house itself were several well-kept fruit trees—mostly fig but some apple. Samson noticed the nice clothes the servants were wearing and wondered if he should've worn more than his work clothes.

They exited the vineyards and began to walk up the hill to the house. 'The land is impressive,' Samson said. 'Why can't our place look like this?'

'We're goat farmers. Goats are messy. It's our goal to turn a profit, not to wow the neighbours with manicured shrubbery and vines.'

'Her servants are better dressed than any back in Israel.'

Malachi smiled. 'Perhaps you should pay us more, sir.'

Samson & the Siren

Samson laughed. 'I guess I set myself up for that one. I shouldn't care what they wear, just so long as they don't turn out to be—'

'Greetings!' a voice called. They looked up and saw a middle-aged man approaching them. 'What can I do for you?' he asked.

'My name is Samson, and this is my servant, Malachi. We received a request to come and discuss a business deal regarding meat.'

'Are you the goat farmer?' the man asked.

Samson smiled and patted the beast on his shoulders. 'Was it the kid that gave it away?'

The man failed to give even a token laugh and bowed politely. 'I am her ladyship's chief manager. As she's expecting you, I'll take you to her at once,' he said and turned towards the house.

'Her ladyship?' Samson mouthed silently to Malachi, who replied with a shrug as they followed the servant up the hill to the house.

Before they entered, the servant turned towards them. 'Please tether the goat with this,' he said, handing them a small rope. 'Her ladyship will come out to see it if she so desires.'

Samson took the goat off his shoulders, and Malachi tethered it to a nearby post. Samson patted his sword and took a deep

The Oliver Anderson Trilogy

breath. If all this were an elaborate trap, he would find out in just a moment.

'Right this way,' the servant said and entered the house.

Samson glanced at Malachi. 'Care for a wager?'

'Over what?'

'Whether we face Philistine thugs or Miss Camel-face.'

Malachi shook his head and sighed. 'They're not thugs, sir.'

'Ok, then you go first.'

'As you wish, sir,' he said, and they stepped out of the daylight into the house.

24

THE FLOORS OF the house were wooden, and the walls, cedar with large, tiled mosaics. Windows filled the reception room with an abundance of light, and fine sofas and tables with luxury goods were everywhere, but not to the point of being gaudy. Whoever this woman was, she had money.

'Please wait here. I'll inform her ladyship that you have arrived,' the servant bowed and exited the room.

'Quite a place,' Samson said.

'How do you mean?'

'Look at this place. They probably imported this furniture from overseas.'

'Still have a love for the Philistine life, sir?' Malachi said, half asking, half remarking.

Samson shrugged his shoulders. He knew his love-hate fascination with Philistine culture was complicated. 'I suppose,'

145

he said. 'I just never understood why Hebrew families like ours have such plain houses by comparison.'

'As you know, they put great value on external appearances, sir. Heaven, by contrast, looks at a man's heart.'

Samson sighed. 'Sounds like something mother would've said—though experience has shown me it's true. Still, it'd be nice if our people could have finer things.'

'We have the Law of Moses and the Ark of the Covenant.'

Samson smiled at his servant. 'Those are great and all, but have you seen this sofa?'

'It does look comfortable, sir.'

'Glad you can admit that much,' Samson said. 'Now, how are we going to get as much Philistine money as possible out of Miss Camel-face?'

'Welcome,' a confident, feminine voice called from across the room. Samson and Malachi turned their heads and saw the lady of the house. She stood for a moment before taking her first step. The man took in the sight of her. Her hair was a dark brown with hints of auburn and her eyes a striking green—a physical quality that didn't exist among the Hebrews and was rare even among the Philistines. She wore a single blue linen garment that was slightly translucent and fastened just beneath her breasts. She wore large earrings and a golden hairband. Her

Samson & the Siren

eyelids were purple, and her lips were a ruby red. She was more beautiful than any woman Samson had seen in a long time.

She seemed to glide effortlessly across the room, keeping eye contact with them as she moved. She approached the men closely and curtsied. 'It's so good to have you in my home.'

Malachi looked over at Samson, expecting him to introduce them, but his master's mouth was hanging open. Finally, after an awkward silence, he took the initiative. 'Hello, your ladyship. My name is Malachi, and this is my master, Samson. We thank you for having us over to discuss the possibility of supplying you and your household with dairy goats and meat,' he said and gave his master a nudge.

'Y-yes, your ladyship,' Samson said, still feasting his eyes on his hostess. 'You-your house is beautiful.'

The lady's lips raised in a slight smile. 'I'm glad you like what you see, my lord Samson. But, please, speak to me as an equal. Call me Delilah.'

'An equal. Delilah. Yeah-yes,' he said as the words tumbled clumsily out of his mouth. Malachi let a snicker slip. 'Thank you for your invitation. I assume you'd like to discuss my meat?'

'Goat meat,' Malachi interjected. 'If I understand correctly.'

Delilah smiled. 'Yes, you understand correctly, good servant. Shall we have a seat here on the sofas, and you can explain to me how your business works?'

The Oliver Anderson Trilogy

'With all due respect, my lady,' Malachi said, 'We've travelled long and are in work clothes. We expected to speak with your servant outside, not recline indoors on your beautiful furniture. Surely the details of our goat business would bore your ladyship.'

'Why do you think I wouldn't take an interest in the meat I eat? Do you assume this because I'm young—or because I'm a woman?'

'Yeah, Malachi,' Samson said, nudging him with his elbow. 'Delilah wants to know about the meat she puts in her mouth. She's a woman of fine taste—let's not rush things.' He turned to her. 'We would be happy to discuss what we can provide.'

Delilah pointed for them to sit on a blue sofa with a silver frame. Samson had a couple of couches in his house, but neither was as lovely or luxurious as this one. Delilah sat across from them on one made of purple fabric and outlined with gold. She locked eyes with Samson. 'So, Samson, tell me about yourself. You are Israeli nobility, correct?'

'Israel doesn't have nobility in the same way Philistia does. We have leaders and wealthy families, but we don't have the same division of class. My own family has been successful in business, goats and fox traps being our main trade.'

'I see,' Delialah said. 'And do all wealthy Israelis dress like you?'

'Hebrew leaders aren't afraid to put on work clothes and labour with their servants. It's part of our culture. In Israel, we are all equal under the law—our God has made the rich and the poor alike,' Samson said. Malachi looked proudly at his master.

'The same god makes both?' she asked. 'What a strange thought. Now that I live near the border, I must learn more about your Hebrew ways.'

'You want to learn about us?' Samson asked. He wondered whether he'd ever heard another Philistine say that. He couldn't remember any—certainly no one from the upper classes.

'I'm hoping some Hebrew neighbour might be willing to explain these things—even if it is to someone as dull and boring as myself.'

'I don't think you're dull at all,' Samson said with an awkward grin.

'Ahem,' Malachi said, clearing his throat. 'I'm sure our good lady will have no trouble finding a nice, Hebrew lady to answer her questions and explain our ways. But we're here to talk about goat meat. Would you like me to explain how we operate, your ladyship?'

'No, Malachi. I've got this,' he said, sitting up straight and turning to Delilah. 'The first question we have is one of quantity. How much meat would you like delivered?'

The Oliver Anderson Trilogy

'My servants and I shall require seven dressed goats a week—one per day.' Delilah said, prompting a smile from both men. Delivering a whole goat already dressed and ready to roast was their most expensive item. Seven per week would make her their biggest client.

'Seven, that's a lot,' Malachi said.

'I have many servants. Are you unable to fulfil my order?' Delilah asked.

'No, my lady,' Samson interjected. 'We'll fill it. Now, about our prices—'

'How about fourteen pieces of silver?' she suggested.

'Per week?' Malachi asked.

'Yes, per week. Two per goat,' Delilah said. 'That's enough, isn't it?'

The men glanced at each other. She was offering twice as much as they'd usually charge. Malachi turned back to Delilah. 'Deal. When would you like your first delivery?'

'In three days,' she said. 'I'd like two to be delivered every other day. Will that be a problem?'

'No, my lady. We'll have a lad deliver two goats every other day as requested,' Malachi said. He had been a servant to Samson's family and their business for forty years and had only once had a client put in an order this big. His mind raced with ideas of what they might put this money towards—widows to support, weapons to buy, and militiamen to pay. 'Is there anything else we can do for you, your ladyship?'

'Yes,' she said, looking straight at Samson, 'I'm hoping that the owner of the business might deliver them in person on the odd occasion—when he's available, of course.'

'Well, I—' Samson began.

'Since I'm new to this area, it's important that I get to know my neighbours, especially those on an equal social footing to myself,' she said and turned to gaze out the window. Her cleavage lifted as she took in a deep breath and slowly exhaled.

'Your ladyship, I'm afraid that won't do,' Malachi said coolly. 'My master is a very busy man. He travels a lot and is often not at the farm. He has more than—'

'I'd love to,' Samson interrupted. 'I've been working a lot lately and need to invest time in making new friends.'

Delilah smiled. 'I'm glad to hear it. I was unsure whether Philistines and Hebrews got along here in the borderlands. I didn't have any Hebrew neighbours back in Gath, you see.'

'It'd be an honour to welcome you to the neighbourhood. I'll bring the meat over myself—maybe once every couple of weeks,' Samson said.

Malachi sighed.

The Oliver Anderson Trilogy

'I hope that, when you do, you shall join me for dinner. Perhaps you could tell me about the area and the greatness of the Hebrews—am I asking too much?'

Samson wiggled on the sofa. 'No-not at all.'

***

They were half a mile from the estate when Malachi finally said, 'May I speak freely, sir?'

'Always,' Samson said. 'Although I know what you're going to say.'

'Then take it to heart. I see danger written all over this. What do we know about this woman?'

'You oversaw the background check. What else is there to know?' Samson asked, staring at his shadow as they trotted along, the setting sun to their backs. 'We have a lovely new neighbour from Gath. She's not involved in any military operations or oppressing our people. Should I treat her like an enemy just because she's a Philistine? Doesn't the Law of Moses say we're supposed to love our neighbours?'

'I'm not sure dinners with beautiful young women is what Moses had in mind.'

Samson laughed. 'What are you afraid of? That she'll attack me with a hunk of goat meat? Are you afraid her servants will beat me up?'

'I'm afraid your eyes are leading you again.'

Samson & the Siren

Samson groaned. 'Now you sound like my moth—'

'Yes, I know I do. And, if I remember correctly, the last time you got involved with an attractive Philistine girl, she warned you about it, you didn't listen to her, and it didn't go so well.'

Samson exhaled through gritted teeth. 'OK, I'll bring her the meat next week, and we'll simply converse. If I sense danger, I'll back off and let the delivery boys bring the meat from then on. OK?'

'I'd been hoping you'd take time off to build friendships. She's not what I had in mind.'

'Yes, mother,' Samson muttered.

The Oliver Anderson Trilogy

25

GOLIATH DISMOUNTED HIS donkey, and the two siblings threw their arms around each other under a fig tree. Delilah squeezed him tight and wouldn't let him go.

'Alright, Dee. I didn't escape the Egyptians only to be suffocated by my big sister.'

She stepped back and looked him up and down. 'Big? I may be your older sister, but I'm certainly not your bigger sister anymore.' He was the same height as a year ago, but his shoulders had broadened. A year of battle on the frontlines had added muscle to the man who was, not long ago, just a boy.

'Come, the servants are finishing the meal. You can tell me all about your year while we eat,' Delilah said.

Goliath smiled from ear to ear. 'Oh no, I'm not going to talk first. You're the one who has explaining to do.'

Delilah looked around at the land and the house. 'Well, yes,' she said with a grin. 'I suppose this does need a bit of explanation. But, first, how long are you here for?' she asked, grabbing his hand and leading him towards their childhood home.

'I can only spend one night. Then I need to get back to Ekron.'

'OK, let's get your donkey some straw,' she said as they approached the house. Delilah waved over a servant to take the beast. Then, as he walked off, she turned and said, 'I'll go first. But I'll keep it short. You're the one who's been in Egypt.'

'Fine. But, before we talk, I want to see my old room!'

***

After a tour of the house and reminiscing on childhood memories, they sat and talked while the servants brought them food. Delilah adored her little brother, but there were some secrets she wouldn't tell even him. He'd worry or be concerned for her honour. She told him the property was now the possession of a general's wife who had hired her to decorate and manage the property, with a team of servants to command.

'Wow!' Goliath remarked, amazed at his sister's good fortune. He washed a hunk of goat down with wine from the estate, 'That's amazing. Does she know this was your childhood home?' Delilah wanted to move on. She was a good liar, but

155

Goliath knew her better than anyone—and thinking up an excuse for how she got the place hadn't been easy.

'You know how often I've prayed to the gods that we'd get our old home back. Where's your faith?'

'OK, Dee, no need to scold me. My faith isn't as strong as yours,' he said.

'You used to pray to the gods when you were a boy.'

'Yeah, well, as you know, life hasn't been easy for us.'

'Which is why we need them all the more,' she replied.

'Funny you say that now. Something strange happened recently that got me thinking I should pray more.'

Delilah was glad the conversation was going off her. 'Tell me all about it,' she said and poured him more wine.

'It was right before I got called back to Philistia. Six of us were on a scouting trip up the Nile river. I'll never forget it. It was hot, humid, and the mosquitoes were devouring us like a hungry man when he gets fresh bread. Well, one minute we were swatting at these nasty little buggers and, the next, Egyptian arrows were raining down on us—we'd walked right into an ambush.'

'Were you injured?' Delilah asked with concerned eyes.

'No, that's just it. I turned around and ran faster than I ever have in my life. I cried to the heavens for help and didn't look back until I was halfway to base.'

156

'And the others?'

Goliath hung his head. 'Three died. The other two were hit and injured but managed to escape with me. I was the only one alive and unharmed.'

Delilah exhaled deeply. His story revived a year's worth of anxiety she'd carried for him. 'To which god did you pray? Dagon?'

'I dunno. I didn't have time to think. I looked up and cried, "Whoever can hear, save me!"'

'I'll thank the goddess. I prayed to her for you each day.'

Goliath smiled. 'Perhaps it was her. Perhaps it was a god I haven't heard about yet. But, whatever, I'm here now.'

'That's another answer to prayer.'

'Well, to thank you for all your prayers—and for not being too terrible a big sister—I brought you back a little something,' Goliath said, pulling a small, silver object out of a small shoulder bag he had next to him and handing it to Delilah.

'Thank you,' Delilah said, taking it and looking at it closely. 'A ring? It's beautiful—and not like any I've seen before. Tell me about it.'

'It's from Egypt. With my final bit of pay, I bought ten of them—though I'm giving you the nicest, of course.'

'It's beautiful. Not at all like what we normally see from the Aegean or anyone here in Philistia.'

The Oliver Anderson Trilogy

'I'm glad you like it,' Goliath said, clearly proud of himself.

'What are you going to do with the other nine? Are you looking for girlfriends? You know what they say about those Ekron girls,' she said with a wink.

Goliath laughed. 'Maybe, but the plan is to resell them back in the city and turn a profit. My new job might pay more than that of a common soldier, but only by a little. Egyptian goods can still sell for a good price—if you know where to take them.'

'OK, but just be careful. I know our long war with Egypt might end soon, but there's still the embargo.'

'Always looking out for me, aren't you sis?'

Delilah smiled. 'Someone's got to. Anyway, tell me about this new job.'

'There's not much to say—and I still don't understand why the military leadership chose me for this role over an injured soldier or someone older. I assist the warden, make sure security is tight, and I oversee the lads who feed the prisoners.'

'Well, I'm glad you got the job,' his sister said with a smile.

'Yeah, me too. I get to be back in Philistia and be only a day's journey from you—plus a pay raise. I guess the gods did answer your prayers.'

'Yes, the gods have been good to us,' Delilah said. She knew she could never tell Goliath the real reason behind his good fortune.

Samson & the Siren

The siblings finished their meal and made their way to the sofas, where they talked. Memories of childhood games and their parents were tossed back and forth like two children playing catch with a leather ball. They stayed up late and slept better than either had in a long time.

The following day, Delilah walked her brother and his donkey out to the end of the vineyard rows. 'So when will you come to see me? I'm afraid my place in Ekron isn't nearly as nice or as spacious as this.'

She smiled. Here was her little brother, all grown up with a career and a place of his own. She knew his job didn't pay much, but it was honest work. That was more than she could say for herself. 'Yes. I can't wait to see your bachelor pad. It's hard for me to get away from here for very long, but I'll come down—maybe in the next month or so.'

They held each other for a long time. Then Goliath mounted his donkey and headed back to his duties in Ekron. She watched him go until he was out of sight.

Then her mind turned towards Samson's next visit.

26

THE MILITIAMEN CHEERED as they removed the covering and looked into the cart. 'Swords! Bows! Spears! Bring on the Philistine filth,' they said as they inspected their new treasure.

'Enjoy them, lads,' Samson said. 'You're holding Hebrew-made weapons.'

Over the last few months, the Philistines had increased their military presence along the border. According to Hebrew intelligence, the two Philistine garrisons in the Sorek Valley had doubled their soldiers and patrols. In response, Samson and the men had raised money for underground blacksmiths instead of only smuggling in Philistine weapons. As a result, two blacksmiths now worked full time in the mountains in the northeast, helping arm their Hebrew brothers with iron weapons.

As they cheered, Malachi approached with a laden donkey. 'Wine and fig cakes to celebrate with, sir?'

'Perfect timing, Malachi, ' Samson replied. 'Lads, have a drink and some pressed figs! Put the swords and spears back first. I don't want any of you dummies swinging a sword around if you're guzzling on a skin of wine,' he said. The men accepted the invitation, laid down their weapons, and took the wineskins to the shade of a nearby tree. They were in good spirits. They didn't know what the Philistines were planning, but they'd be ready with new weapons and Samson as their captain.

And Yahweh. They mustn't forget they had Him too.

'Now that you have these, what'll be the next step?' Malachi asked.

'A raid,' Samson said. 'Food and other supplies come to the garrisons from Ekron twice a week.'

'And what would be the reason for these raids, sir?'

'The first reason is to take their supplies as payment for our men and their families.'

'And the other reason?'

Samson smiled. 'Cut off their food, and the soldiers go hungry. Hungry soldiers don't fight so well.'

Malachi took a deep breath. 'Does that mean you're planning an all-out attack on a Philistine garrison?'

The Oliver Anderson Trilogy

'Have a drink, Malachi. We want Philistine soldiers out of the Sorek. We don't mind peaceful Philistines living here, but stationed soldiers make our nation vulnerable. So at some point, yes, we'll have to take on the garrisons.'

Malachi cringed. He knew a direct attack on a garrison would lead to open war. 'Aren't there other garrisons that pose a threat to our nation besides the ones here in Sorek?'

'Of course. But our priority is Dan—our militias can't cover all twelve of Israel's tribes. The men of Judah and Benjamin will have to see to themselves down south. In the north, well Eli is stationed at Shiloh,' Samson said hesitantly.

'You don't trust Eli, do you, sir?'

'Eli is OK as a priest, but his leadership for the region is weak. And, if what I hear about his sons is correct, well, let's just say they lack the integrity priests should have.'

'Yes, leaders should have integrity, shouldn't they, sir?'

Samson bore his gaze into Malachi. 'Are you implying anything by that comment?'

Malachi glanced over at the men under the tree. He knew they were distant and jubilant enough not to overhear what he was about to say. 'I'm worried, sir. I'm grateful for the extra income we've received from our newest Philistine client over the last three months, but I worry for you.'

Samson & the Siren

Samson lifted a spear from the cart and held it in his hands as if to inspect it. 'Why should you worry about me, Malachi?'

'You know why, sir. Every couple of weeks, you disappear for two or three days. I'm worried that being involved with a Philistine woman might compromise your role as judge and leader. You're needed here.'

'I fulfil my duties. Look, these men are happy and equipped. We're ready for whatever the Philistines might plan.'

'Perhaps I'm overly overcautious. I hope so. But, in my experience, when something comes our way from Philistia that looks too good to be true, it usually is. Oppression can come at a man wrapped in all sorts of packages.'

Samson smiled. 'Do you think her ladyship is oppressing me?'

'I do not know her intentions, sir. I'm concerned that she meets with you with no appranet talk of marriage.'

'You want me to marry a Philistine, Malachi?'

'No, sir. I'd much prefer you marry a daughter of Israel— although, if she were to convert to Israel and her God, I would find that acceptable. But marriage is at least repectable. This women, if she doesn't even speak of marriage, what does she want?'

'I tried marriage once—didn't work out so well.'

The Oliver Anderson Trilogy

'She lacked integrity. If Delilah has integrity and is willing to convert, it will be different. But, if she has no integrity to speak of, why waste your precious time on her?'

'Because she makes me feel... alive.' Samson said. 'Delilah admires me, not as a leader or a warrior—she knows nothing about that. She admires me as me. She enjoys my company, and I enjoy hers. I think I'm beginning to, to—'

'Love her, sir?'

Samson lifted the wineskin to his lips and took a swig. 'Yes, I suppose,' he said.

'Then at least marry her. If she is willing to convert, this union might at least become righteous before God.'

'There are two reasons I can't.'

'And what are they, sir?'

'She doesn't know about...' Samson spread his arms about, pointing to the weapons and the men, 'all this.'

'Your fighting? Ah, fair point, sir.'

'If I were to marry her, she would soon learn I'm more than just a goat farmer. How would she feel if she knew I did battle against Philistine soldiers?'

'I understand your hesitancy. Even if Lady Delilah is not especially patriotic or politically minded, that could be hard to swallow. And the other reason?'

Samson looked over at the men. 'Them.'

Samson & the Siren

'Them, sir?'

'Some of them wouldn't understand if I were to have a Philistine wife—even if she did profess the faith of Israel. And, as to that point of faith, I've never brought up the subject. I doubt it's crossed her mind.'

'The only way your relationship with her ladyship has any chance of lasting is if she's willing to accept your militia activities and convert to Israel. Sooner or later, she's going to know the full truth about you. If you're not willing to deal with these issues, why continue this relationship? It'll only be doomed to failure.'

Samson knew he was right. 'I know all this. I just don't want to lose her.'

Malachi looked at his master with compassion. He could remember what it was to feel in love. 'Of course, you don't, sir. You feel as if she's cured you of your loneliness and opened up a whole new world of excitement. What I'm telling you is hard, but it's for your good that I speak. It would best if you left her altogether but, if your heart is that set on the girl, at least persuade her to convert and marry you.'

'OK.'

'OK?'

'I'll tell her about my activities and ask her if she's open to marriage—a Hebrew marriage,' Samson said.

The Oliver Anderson Trilogy

'And if she's not?'

A look of irritation flashed across his face. 'That's not an option I care to entertain right now!'

'But it's possible.'

'No, I *will* convince her that this is for the best... for us. It may take some time, but I'll persuade her.'

Malachi placed his hand on his master's back. He'd faithfully cared for Samson since he was a boy. 'Your parents wanted me to look out for you, sir. I wouldn't be doing my duty if I was silent.'

Samson smiled and embraced his elderly servant. 'I know, Malachi—and that's just one of a thousand reasons why I love you.'

27

ELISE SIGHED. 'STUPID man. Can't he see what she's doing to him?'

'Many a man has been rendered weak and witless in the presence of a beautiful woman,' Grandpa William quipped.

'Perhaps. But I think most women want a strong man—not one who is led astray easily,' Elise.

'Good women like strong men,' Grandpa replied. 'But there are other women who prefer weak men—they're easier to control that way.'

'Yes,' Elise said. 'But those women aren't happy. Deep down, we desire to have a competent man.'

Oliver cleared his throat, 'Well, just call me Mr Competent, baby.'

Elise laughed. 'You're doing OK, I suppose.'

'Aw, thanks. You make me feel like a top-tier bloke.'

The Oliver Anderson Trilogy

'Anytime,' Elise said with a wink.

'When you went out to the toilet, grandpa told me something interesting.'

'Oh?'

'Yeah, he explained how different Southern American Christians reacted during the days of Jim Crow laws.'

'Any chance I could hear it?'

'I'll explain it to you this evening,' Oliver said. 'Grandpa, one thing you mentioned was how many Christians believed the social distancing of blacks and whites was wrong, but that they still went along with it because the government said so.'

'Yes, they did,' William replied. 'That was an example of when Christians submitted in a way they shouldn't have. Of course, there are passages in the Bible that speak about submission to civil authority. I can think of Romans 13 and 1 Peter 2.'

'So how did churches and ministers who fought against either Jim Crow or Eastern European Communism come to terms with those passages?'

'Christian dissidents give lots of thought to those passages—along with other parts of the Bible. In Acts 5, for example, the Apostles declared, "It is better to obey God rather than men".'

'How should we know what laws to resist?' Elise asked.

Samson & the Siren

'St. Augustine said that an unjust law is no law at all. Christ calls us to follow him even when some of the practical outworkin' of that obedience might break human law.'

'So we're anarchists?' Oliver asked

'Not at all!' William said firmly. 'God has ordained human government. When it behaves as it should, it's glorious. When it fails to do what it should—or when it attempts to do somethin' beyond its remit—that's when we have problems.'

'What do you mean by "remit"?'

'Good question, Elise. Ye see, God has all authority, but he delegates some of that authority to us. Parents, for example, have limited authority over their children. Bosses have limited authority over their employees, and pastors have limited authority in their churches. Likewise, the government has authority, but it's limited?'

'How's it limited?' Oliver asked.

'A pastor doesn't have the authority to command his people what clothes they should wear around the house. A parent can't tell their teenage children to drive 30 miles per hour above the speed limit. To know the limits of any human authority, one must first ask what the purpose of that authority is. God gives humans authority to fulfil a purpose. The moment a parent, or pastor, or government begins to issue dictates outside of its

The Oliver Anderson Trilogy

callin', it becomes tyrannical. That's when Christians should resist.'

'By "resist", you mean....'

'I'm not talkin' about anythin' violent. I mean peaceful civil disobedience. I can't obey a man-made law that my conscience can't reconcile with the God of Scripture.'

'Thanks for explaining that, grandpa,' Elise said. 'It's helpful for me as I think about this MAGBT teacher.'

'Do you know what you'll say to her yet?' Oliver asked, placing his hand on top of hers.

'No, not yet—but thoughts are beginning to form. Anyway, can you tell me more about Samson and his honey trap?'

'Of course, lassie,' William said. 'Samson was fallin' in love, alright. But not everyone thought Delilah's seduction was goin' fast enough.'

Samson & the Siren

28

DELILAH SAT BY the window overlooking the estate. Her right hand clasped a cup of cool, fermented goat's milk. She wrapped herself in nostalgia like a warm blanket as her eyes went to and from across the landscape—with every tree and hill calling forth childhood memories.

That she was back here in the Sorek was a dream come true. The mountains surrounding the valley felt to her to be a giant wall of protection from the harsh realities of Philistine life and politics that transpired in the cities. She sighed and took a sip of milk. *What would life have been like had the soldiers never come for us? What if Goliath and I had grown up here—under the caring watch of our parents?* She imagined their father training Goliath to run the family business and her parents working together to find a good and loving man that she could marry.

As her mind drifted through the lands of *What If,* she noticed a group making their way through the woods towards the estate. She leaned forward and stared into the distance until she could make out who it might be.

Crap! They were Philistine soldiers.

She knew it wouldn't be her brother. Goliath wouldn't bring fellow soldiers home without giving her ample warning. Her hand tightened on her cup. 'Please don't let it be Achish,' she whispered.

The general marched up the hill with his detachment of soldiers around him. It had been almost three months since he'd sent Delilah and eight of his best soldiers to the estate to engage in espionage—and he was eager to see if his investment had anything to show for it.

As they approached the house, he turned to his men. 'Wait here and keep guard. Be on the alert for anyone approaching the estate.' He began to walk to the house when the front door swung open.

'What are you doing here, General?' Delilah asked, her eyes flashing.

He stopped. 'Hello, my dear,' he said. 'We were just a few miles away, securing our ever-growing garrison, and I thought

Samson & the Siren

'I'd come by to make sure you were being taken care of and to see how you were getting on.'

'I've sent you updates by messenger twice. You have all the information you need,' Delilah said, looking down at him from the porch, her hands firmly planted on her hips.

'I know. And the messengers have given me full reports on both occasions. But, as I was nearby, I thought I'd see it all with my own eye. Ensuring your safety and welfare is my top priority,' Achish said as he slowly resumed his approach.

'Hm, and yet, you coming here doesn't make me feel especially safe for some reason.'

'Let's let the past be the past, my dear. We're partners now.'

Delilah crossed her arms. 'Partners?'

'Yes, something like that. We're working together for the good of the nation, and we'll both benefit from this project long-term—if it works. Now, come, allow me in, and perhaps you can answer a few of the questions I have about how everything is going. I promise I won't stay long.'

As much as she hated Achish, Delilah couldn't deny that life had improved for her and her brother thanks to him. 'Fine, come in,' she said as she turned and marched into the house.

Achish followed after her through the entranceway and down the hall into the main sitting room. He looked about carefully. 'Nice décor. I like what you've done with the place.'

'You didn't come all this way so we can chat about home furnishings.'

'You are correct,' Achish said as he walked over to the purple sofa and sat with his legs crossed. 'As I said, I thought we could have a friendly conversation about how life is for you and how our project is progressing. Might we share a drink?'

'A drink, really?'

'Come, there is no need for hostility between us.'

'No need for—' Delilah began but bit her tongue. She knew it wouldn't serve her to yell at him. She took a deep breath and said, 'OK, a drink. What would you like?'

'I hear the wine on this estate is lovely.'

'Yes, the family that kept this vineyard did great things with wine,' she said with an accusing eye and turned to fetch her unwelcome visitor a drink.

As she moved about the room, Achish's eye danced up and down her body. He was used to having beautiful women, but Delilah's natural physique and fiery attitude made her exceptionally desirable. For a moment, he considered raping her. And why not? He'd done so before. He could force himself on her here on the sofa. She wasn't an aristocrat wife or daughter, so there'd be no consequences with the Philistine lords.

Samson & the Siren

But, as she brought him his wine, he decided against it. It's not that he had any moral qualms about raping her—she was, after all, a whore whose parents were traitors. But he wanted her body *and* her spirit. Acquiring that would take a more delicate sort of manipulation.

He smiled. 'Thank you for the drink. Aren't you going to have something?'

Delilah stood in the centre of the room. 'Let's get to business. Just ask your questions and leave.'

'My dear, have I failed to live up to my end of the deal? Are you finding your servants or accommodation unsatisfactory in some way?'

Delilah paused to think before answering. 'No,' she said, loathing the man but feeling a need to be fair. 'You've kept your side of the bargain, and I a—' she struggled to get the word out, 'appreciate that. The house is as lovely as I remember it, and the soldier-servants you provided have respected my privacy and managed the estate without fault.'

'Thank you. I know you may not like me much because of what my job required me to do so many years ago, but I'd hate to think that I wasn't doing right by you now.'

Delilah wasn't sure how to respond. The man she'd hated all of these years was the same one letting her live in the one place she wanted to be more than anywhere else. 'You are doing right

The Oliver Anderson Trilogy

by me. *Now*, at least. But don't ever expect me to forget that you're the man responsible for killing my parents.'

'I doubt anything I say would adequately convey the sincerity of my regret.'

'You're right about *that*, General.'

'It's Achish,' he said tenderly. 'Sometimes, in war, men are sent out to do unpleasant jobs based on orders from their superiors. People, even good people, get hurt.'

'Were your orders to violate me? To burn my parents to death?'

Achish bowed and shook his head. 'It was at a time when Egypt was buying up spies and assets. The Lords entrusted me with the responsibility of keeping our people safe.'

Delilah's eyes flashed fire. 'My parents weren't in the pay of Egypt!'

'I'm afraid evidence came to light that suggested the contrary. Please understand that everything I did was to protect our people from the jaws of Egypt—because I love our country. You don't want Egypt to wipe us out, do you?'

'Well, no, but—'

'Sometimes, harsh things happen in war, and otherwise good people commit unfortunate acts. But let's not discuss the past anymore. Instead, I've come to talk about the present—about our partnership.'

Samson & the Siren

'Hm, there's that word again.'

'Now, my main question is simply: where are we with Samson? I'm glad you've managed to establish a relationship and that he's visiting you regularly. But has he given any clues concerning the secret of his strength?'

'I can make a man desire me quickly. But trust takes time to build with anyone—especially with someone who's been hurt.'

'Hurt by his dead wife, you mean? Yes, I understand—and I don't mean to pressure you.'

Delilah sat on the sofa opposite him. 'You were correct about his loneliness. He doesn't simply swing by for sex as if I was a common whore. Instead, he seems to be falling in love with me,' she said professionally.

Achish grinned. 'Wonderful! And you're sure of this?'

'You know how I operate. I've made many men fall in love with me. It's not just the tricks I perform in bed. I get them to share the most personal details of their lives until they believe that I understand them better than anyone.'

'And this is what Samson is doing?'

'The last time he was here, he wept when he recounted to me the death of his parents,' Delilah said with a proud smile.

Achish took another sip of his wine, and said, 'Well done, Delilah. I knew that it wasn't a mistake to choose you. Let me convey that not only I, but all of the Philistine Lords are exceptionally proud of you.'

'They—the Lords—they're aware of what I'm doing?' she asked, surprised.

'Oh yes. I've conveyed your bravery and willingness to accept this dangerous assignment for the good of the nation. You're a hero.'

'A hero?' she asked aloud to herself. Delilah had connections with men in power but never as high as one of the seven Philistine lords. 'Thank you for conveying my work to them, General,' she said, uncomfortable with the sense of appreciation she felt.

'It's Achish. Now, how are we going to find out the secret of Samson's strength?'

'I'll ask him. Soon. I'm simply waiting for the right moment when the question will seem natural to him.'

'When it does come, communicate with the soldiers I've given you. If the source of his strength is something you can deal with yourself, like reciting some spell, feel free to take the initiative. If you can't handle it, send a soldier for me at once, and we will do whatever is necessary to break the man.'

'I understand.'

Samson & the Siren

'The Hebrew militias have gotten more aggressive lately. Just last week, they interrupted a food delivery from Ekron. The sooner we can eliminate their captain, the better.'

'I won't take longer than necessary, but I can't give him any reason to suspect me.'

Achish took a final gulp of his wine and stood. 'I understand. One must do these things delicately. That's why I'm glad the nation has you. I know you'll find that perfect moment.' He walked over and handed her the empty cup.

She took it and stood. 'Thank you for your trust, Achish.'

'Now, you expressed that you did not want me to stay for long. I want to show you that I respect your wishes and your privacy, so I shall leave you now,' he said and turned to walk to the door.

Delilah followed him, cautiously noting his gentlemanly behaviour. 'Thank you for respecting my boundaries.'

He reached the door and turned his gaze to hers. 'Well, it is your home. It's the least I could do,' he said. Then he leaned in and kissed her on the forehead. 'Goodbye, my dear.'

Delilah watched as the general and his soldiers walked downhill and into the Sorek valley until they were out of sight amidst its twists and turns. *That was interesting,* she thought. She turned back inside, went to her bathroom, and scrubbed her forehead.

The Oliver Anderson Trilogy

29

THEY PULLED THE linen sheets over their bodies as their heavy breathing began to return to normal. The lovers had shared dinner and a long conversation and then retired to the bedroom where they'd enjoyed each other. Now her head was resting on his chest.

Delilah had slept with more men than she could remember. She found Samson, for all the talk of him being a mighty warrior, to be average in the bedroom—even if he was warmer and more tender than most. She knew how to adjust her performances to her clients' needs. With Samson, she'd spent the evening laughing at all his cavalier jokes and listening while he opened and shared more of his past. Delilah, likewise, had recounted more from the cover story that she and Achish had established—having to make some details up on the fly.

Samson & the Siren

Samson was sincerely amazed by Delilah. She was everything he longed for in a lover. Yes, she looked terrific, especially naked, and he was amazed at how Delilah could anticipate his movements and bodily rhythms when they made love. But he also felt like he truly knew her and that she knew him. He was in love—and the thought of losing this new treasure scared him.

He caressed her head as it rose and fell with his breathing. 'I love you, Delilah.'

'Mm,' she purred. 'I love you too.'

'I want you to have all of me, and I want to have all of you.'

'Sounds wonderful, my love. What do you have in mind?'

'I think we should marry.'

Marriage? Delilah wasn't quite expecting that. Still, she had been proposed to by clients before and felt she could use this development to her advantage. 'Marriage is a big step. Are you unhappy with having me as a lover?'

'No, not at all. It's just that—'

'Just what?'

'I want to know you even better than I do. I want to share my life on the other side of the valley with you. I want us to raise children together.'

'Children? Do you think we know each other well enough?'

'What's there to know? We love each other. We'll get to know each other better after we're married.'

181

Delilah sat up. 'What would my life in Israel be like if I married you? What does the wife of a Hebrew goat farmer do all day?'

Samson grinned. 'You mean besides raising children?' he said. 'Well, support me in my work.'

'And what does your goat work entail?'

Samson paused to think one last time whether he was ready to divulge his other activities to Delilah. He knew he needed to do it if any talk of marriage was to be genuine. 'There is one thing I haven't told you about me.'

Delilah raised her eyebrows. 'Oh?'

'Yes, I'm sorry. I've wanted to tell you. It's just that, well, I've been afraid I might lose you if you knew.'

'I love you, Samson. You being open only makes me love you more.'

Samson nodded. 'I agree. We should be honest, but this is different.'

'Try me,' she said with a grin.

'Do you know how the Philistine soldiers have treated my people? They've robbed and oppressed us—and continue to this day.'

'I've heard some things. Before moving here, I didn't pay any attention to those sorts of politics.'

Samson & the Siren

'Have you heard of Hebrew militias that sometimes get into skirmishes with Philistine soldiers?'

'I've heard such things, yes.'

'How would you feel if you knew I was involved in those militias?'

Delilah paused. Her mind raced with possible ways to respond to his disclosure—determining which would get her quickest to her goal. 'I know,' she said finally.

'Really?'

'Samson, do you think I could live here for four months and not hear about the mighty Samson, the captain of the Hebrew militia?'

Samson sat up. 'How long have you known?'

'For a while.'

'Why didn't you bring it up?'

'Because,' Delilah said, sitting up. 'I wanted to see if you would trust me enough to tell me on your own.'

Samson exhaled deeply as he leaned back against the pillows. The fact that she knew, and had known for some time, sent his mind spinning. 'So... how do you feel now that I've told you?'

She smiled. 'Look, my love. You and I are both sitting here in the bed facing each other. Naked. I want us to be naked relationally. No secrets. If we're even to begin talking about

The Oliver Anderson Trilogy

marriage, I must know we have no more secrets from each other.'

'Yes, this is what I want!' Samson said, bouncing on the bed like an excited boy. 'I want us to know and accept each other fully. But doesn't it bother you that I fight against your countrymen?'

'You know me, Samson. I'm not especially political. As long as I know that you're only fighting soldiers that have passed into Israel, well, I can live with that. I know Philistine soldiers can be overly aggressive. You guys are simply fighting defensive battles.'

'Yes!' he said, wanting to justify himself in her eyes. 'We never attack Philistine women or children—and avoid civilians as much as possible.'

Delilah nodded. 'I understand. Leading a defensive militia doesn't make me want to leave you. In fact,' she said, rubbing her hand along his leg, 'it makes it a bit exciting.'

Samson had rehearsed this disclosure many times in his head, but this was going better than expected. 'This is brilliant! I'm so glad you see it that way. I want you to know all about me so that, when we do marry, there'll be no surprises.'

'I do have one question.'

'Ask it. There's nothing I'd keep from you.'

Samson & the Siren

Delilah found it hard to suppress a smile. 'I hear that, when you engage in battle, your strength is unequalled. How did you become such a mighty fighter?'

'The God I serve gives me strength.'

'I can believe it. But how does it work?'

'When I need it, it just comes. I feel his wrath burn against those who terrorise his people—and that fury flows through me.'

'Is there anything you must do to activate it or keep it?'

'No. It's a gift God told my parents about before I was born—though I didn't discover it until I was a young man.'

'So, if I understand you correctly, you will be strong like this forever? That there's no way for you to lose this power?'

'Well...' Samson began but then hesitated.

'Well?'

'There might be something I could do, but that's between my God and me.'

'So, there is a way you could lose this strength.'

'Maybe. But it's not something I speak about.'

Delilah folded her arms beneath her breasts and turned from him. 'Hmpf! That's what I thought: a man of secrets. I didn't think I could trust you.'

Samson looked down at the bunched up sheets that lay between them. His whole life, he'd kept the secret he'd

The Oliver Anderson Trilogy

inherited from his parents. His fighting men didn't even know this secret. He bit his bottom lip and looked back up at her. 'It's just one of those things, Delilah. It's not that I don't trust you—I've never told anyone about the details of Heaven's call on my life.'

A wounded look flashed across Delilah's face. 'I see how it is. "It's just one of those things"? Please,' she said, emanating cold vibes. 'As you said, if we're to marry, we can't keep secrets. Perhaps this should be our last night together.'

Samson looked into her eyes, heart racing. The suggestion that they'd say goodbye that very night terrified him. 'The secret of my strength comes from Heaven, but I can lose it. If you do one thing, I'll become as weak as any man.'

Delilah smiled. 'I knew we could trust each other.'

186

Samson & the Siren

30

SAMSON HATED LYING to her. He'd thought he was ready to share everything with Delilah. But this secret was sacred—and there wasn't much in his life that was sacred. Samson wasn't as devout as he knew he ought to be: he didn't pray often, and he knew a truly righteous man wouldn't have his uncontrolled sex life. But to betray the secret the angel had given his parents? No. That was the one thing that made him God's man—the one line he could not cross.

He looked over the bedsheets and straight into her eyes. 'If someone ties me up with seven fresh bowstrings that haven't been dried, I'll become as weak as any man.' It was the first idea that flashed through his mind—mainly because he had been constructing new bows with some guys from the militia that very morning.'

'Fresh bowstrings?' Delilah asked. 'Hebrew magic is strange.'

Samson rolled over on his side and exhaled deeply. 'Yes, we have strange ways. I'll tell you more tomorrow.'

Delilah caressed his back. 'Thank you for telling me, my love. I feel closer to you already.'

Samson rubbed his hand through his hair. 'Yeah. It's not something I like to talk about. I guess you can understand why.'

She nodded. 'Of course. As your woman, I'll guard your secret like my very life,' she said with all the appearances of sincerity and conviction.

'I know,' he said. He curled up under the sheets as guilt weighed heavy on him. He hated lying to the woman he was in love with and wondered if he'd done the right thing. *Would it be so wrong to tell her? After all, she is going to be my wife.* He trusted her. But there was a small voice inside him telling him he needed to guard this—even from her.

Samson wrestled with his thoughts until his mind sunk into the oblivion of sleep. His sleep was so deep that he didn't hear his beloved's footsteps as she snuck out of bed and fetched one of her servants.

***

"Samson! Samson!'

The words hit him like small pebbles pelting his face. He groaned as his eyes opened to the sunlight coming in through the east-facing window. *How much wine did I drink last night?*

'Samson!'

'Huh? What is it?' he asked as he tried to turn over in bed to face her voice. When he did, he felt his arms strangely stuck behind him as if both were asleep or like someone was sitting on them. He rolled over to face the ceiling, but he couldn't move his arms.

'Samson!'

He turned his head to see Delilah sitting on a stool by the door. 'What's the matter, my love? Something's wrong with my arms—I'm stuck on something.' He grunted and tried to wiggle himself free.

'Samson, quick! Philistine soldiers are coming towards the house.'

Her words jolted him. 'What? Here, now? How dare they!' Rage took hold of him, and his heart began to thud. The same soldiers that had killed and raped his people now dared to come against him and his lover in the early morning hours?

He lept to his feet and ripped the restraints from his arms. He stood, naked, on the bed with his fists in front of him, ready for a fight. 'What direction are they coming from?'

Delilah stared at him in awe. She'd heard about the phenomenon of his might in battle, but this was the first time she'd seen it. Her body trembled, knowing the arms that had just broken those bonds could just as easily tear her apart.

189

Delilah briefly lost her breath, wondering if she'd committed a major error in judgment.

'Where are they? They will not touch you or enter this house!' he roared.

With one hand over her mouth, she extended the other and pointed to the strands of fresh bowstrings now scattered across the bed and one the floor. Samson's eyes followed her finger, 'Huh… what is all this?'

'I-I' Delilah had prepared her words hours earlier, but now, sitting before his naked might, found it harder to say them. 'I wanted to know if we could trust each other.'

Samsom looked up at her and then back down at the bowstrings. It took a moment for the mental pieces of the puzzle to come together. Finally, he sighed, sat down on the side of the bed, and looked over at her. 'A test? You put me to the test?'

'Of course, Samson, my love. What else could I do? Your talk of marriage last night overwhelmed me,' she said and crossed her arms as if offended.

'So you tied my arms with bowstrings?'

'Fresh ones, just as you said. Ha! Not that it matters now. We can both see perfectly well that you weren't honest with me,' she said in her best scorned-woman voice.

'Wait… you're mad at *me*?'

Samson & the Siren

'And why shouldn't I be?'

'I dunno, I guess 'cause you're the one who tied me up?'

'I needed to test your love and honesty. Any woman would've done the same.'

'Any woman? Really?'

'Obviously! You still have much to learn about how to make the feminine heart feel secure.'

'So *you* tied *me* up... but I'm the one who did something wrong?'

How can you ever expect me to go off and live among the Hebrews as your wife when you can't even tell me the truth.'

Samson realised he'd been caught in his lie and knew it would be hard to explain away. Still, he was surprised she'd gone so far as to test him on it. He wanted to ask where she'd gotten fresh bowstrings from in the middle of the night, but he didn't want to provoke her furry any further. 'Look, dear, I'm sorry. I know I wasn't fully candid with you last night about my strength, but that's because it's a secret I've inherited from my parents. It's a secret known by myself and God alone.'

Delilah stood and looked down at him. 'Fine. You are perfectly entitled to your little secrets. Just don't be surprised if I seem less confident next time you bring up the notion of marriage—because it's clear we understand relationships very differently,' she said as she turned and left the room.

191

Samson remained seated on the bed. Anxiety began pumping through his veins as he contemplated losing her.

Meanwhile, Delilah tip-toed downstairs and instructed her soldier-servants, who were waiting downstairs, to put their swords away. Today would not be the day they capture their prey.

Samson & the Siren

31

'SO WHY IS it taking so long?' the general asked, sitting on the sofa in the Sorek sitting room.

'Like I already told you: he keeps lying,' Delilah said.

'But I thought you said he was in love with you.'

Delilah groaned. 'He is.'

'And how do you know?'

'He says he wants to marry me and sweep me away to Israel.'

Achish watched as she paced back and forth, wringing her hands. Three times she'd asked Samson the secret of his strength, and three times he'd lied to her—lies that were exposed only after she tested them. Achish knew she was taking her mission seriously and that her inability to manipulate the truth out of Samson was exasperating her—especially as she was used to getting what she wanted out of men.

He lifted the wine to his lips. Achish found her attractive when flustered. The sudden movements her body made and the lack of her usual control over her facial expression were a turn-on: he was seeing her in a vulnerable state.

He again resisted the urge to force himself on her. Such a deed might satisfy a momentary appetite, but it wouldn't ensure that he had her for the long term—and that's what he was after. To Achish, she was a game to be won, a novel challenge. *A woman whose parents and virginity I destroyed as a child—can I make her long for me?* As he watched her facing a potential failure, the master manipulator knew what move to make.

'My dear, I know you've tried hard. Truly. But the patience of the Philistine Lords is growing thin. You've been here six months with nothing to show for it. They're wondering how much more time and money they need to give you before their investment pays off,' he said.

'I've tried! OK?' she said, turning to face him. 'I've worked on him emotionally, relationally, sexually—everything I can imagine. I even pretend to be interested in marrying him, and still, he won't tell me.'

'I've done what I can to reassure the Lords that you're doing your best and that it's only a matter of time.'

Delilah took a deep breath. 'And… did they accept that?'

'Some did. Some didn't. But I insisted that they give you more time.'

'Thanks, Achish,' she said—and meant it. 'How much more time do I have?'

Achish bowed his head and breathed out heavily as he thought quickly about how to best respond. 'A month,' he said, looking back up at her.

Delilah took a step back. 'Only one month?'

Achish stood and walked towards her, gently placing his hand on her shoulder. 'You're a gifted woman, Delilah. I know you can do this.'

She began to reach her hand up, to lay it on top of his, but then thought the better of it. Instead, she brushed his off. 'I've tried everything.'

He took a step back, granting her a few more inches of personal space, but kept his eye latched onto her. 'You can do this. I believe in you, Delilah. But, if you don't—if the mission is unsuccessful—then they'll take it all back.'

Delilah looked around the room and out the window towards the vineyards. 'It was wonderful while it lasted—being back here. I hate having to leave it again.'

'Let me guess... you'd rather be here than in the finest mansion in Gath or Ekron. Is that it?'

The Oliver Anderson Trilogy

She liked having someone else near her to articulate what she felt so profoundly. 'Yes, that's it. But this life isn't a wish shop. Not even those who pray to the gods don't keep all their blessings. The gods give, and then the gods take away. Damn them all.'

'A beautifully cynical observation, my dear,' Achish quipped. 'Once this is all over, where will you go?'

'I don't know. My old client network is in Gath, but my brother is in Ekron. I'll have enough money for a nice home in either place.'

'About that...' Achish began.

Delilah's brow furrowed. 'About what?'

'The money. It seems the Lords will interpret a failure to secure the information as a breach of contract. They will expect their money back, minus expenses you might have incurred over the last six months, which, as we've paid for all your servants here, are probably minimal.'

'What? That's not fair!' she said, utterly frustrated. 'I've tried my best. They can't just withhold my salary. I gave up my clients to do this!'

'I know.' Achish said. 'I don't think it's right. But the Lords have a funny way of deciding for themselves what is and isn't fair. I will petition them, but there's more you need to know.'

Samson & the Siren

Delilah stepped back. Her face was white. 'I don't think I want to hear this, do I?'

'It's your brother. They only put him in his current role as part of your package. They think having such a young soldier serve as an assistant warden isn't ideal and that, as a young man, should serve on the front lines.'

'No!'

'Unfortunately, it's true. If this mission fails, they'll send Goliath back to war—maybe this time to face the Hebrew militias.'

Delilah collapsed on the sofa nearest her. The thought of her brother being back in harm's way, this time possibly facing off against some of Samson's men, was more than she could take. She buried her face in the cushions and began to sob.

Achish smiled. Delilah's reactions were all going according to his plan. A tingle of pride rippled down his back at the thought of winning her soul. He stared at her exposed waist as her body convulsed with sobbing and imagined making love to her. *Not now,* he told himself with restraint. Slowly, he sat beside her and once again placed his hand on her shoulder. 'I know this comes as bad news, my dear. But, please, don't be afraid. You can still succeed in this mission. Don't let a fear of failure overwhelm you.'

The Oliver Anderson Trilogy

She placed her hand on top of his. In the face of this bad news, she was open to encouragement from anyone. 'You think so?'

'Yes. I even have something that might help you.'

She turned and sat up so that their bodies were touching, shoulder to shoulder. 'How?' she asked desperately. 'I'll try anything.'

'In the army, we have different ways of interrogating people. Pain, of course, is the easiest option. We have all sorts of instruments we break our subjects with.'

'You want me to torture Samson? I don't think I coul—'

Achish's laugh interrupted her. 'No—not at all. I'm saying that pain doesn't work for everyone, so sometimes we drug them. It confuses the mind and loosens the lips. It doesn't work on everyone, and it's important to get the dosage right. But, if you want to try, I have some I could give you. You could put it in his wine if you wish—it mixes well with that.'

Delilah's mouth dropped open. 'A drug that loosens lips? Yes, of course, I'll try it.'

'I have some outside, with my men and our supplies. Shall I fetch some?'

Delilah's face lit up. 'Yes!' she said and threw her arms around him. She held him for a couple of seconds and then abruptly let go and scooted back a couple of inches. 'Yes, please,

198

General,' she said, looking down at the floor. 'Teach me to use it. It sounds like the only chance we have of completing our mission.'

Our mission? Achish was delighted to see the struggle within her. He'd successfully confused her feelings towards him. 'Of course, I'm on your side. Above all, I want you to be successful and have the life you deserve.'

'Thank you, Gen—Achish.'

'I simply have one request.'

'What's that?' she asked, afraid that his offer of help might be costly.

'I'm based at the garrison just a few miles away, where I'm preparing things for the next general. I can get here quickly. Once you've used the drug and you know his secret, send word to me. Samson has cost me many men now, and I'd like to be here when we get the better of him.'

Delilah lowered her shoulders and relaxed. She was no longer sure how to be around Achish—but his request seemed reasonable. Part of her even wanted him to be here and witness it should she succeed. 'Yes, I'll send you word. He'll probably come again next week.'

Achish stood up. 'Good. I won't be far. Now, I'll get the drug, and we can rehearse how to use it best, OK?'

199

She reached over from the sofa and squeezed his hand. 'Thank you, Achish.'

Achish smiled back. 'You're welcome,' he said and walked out of the house to fetch his poison.

Delilah watched as he walked through the door. When he was gone, a thought shot through her mind. 'He just saved me,' she whispered.

32

THE EMOTIONAL TEMPERATURE in the Sorek living room was looking up at zero. Delilah was, of course, great at communicating her displeasure in non-verbal, passive-aggressive ways, and the message was getting through to Samson loud and clear: his woman wasn't happy. Samson could deal with a dozen violent men. But anger from the woman who held his heart? He didn't know what to do with that.

It started when he entered to greet her. She turned her head so that his kiss landed on her cheek instead of her lips. He tried to embrace her, but her arms didn't return the hold. When he asked her if she was OK, he got the enigmatic response men throughout the ages have heard.

'I'm fine,' she said.

Samson knew what was wrong. Tension had been building as she had repeatedly asked about his strength. Three times he'd given her a fake response, and three times she'd exposed it as such. She was angry and, though his calm exterior was slow to show it, he was getting scared. Behind his bold and playful demeanour lay plenty of insecurity when it came to women. He feared Delilah's anger might lead her to call it quits—and, for some reason not fully understood by even him, that idea terrified him. In a relatively short period, she'd managed to fill an emotional hole that he'd only been partially aware existed.

'You're still mad about, you know, last time?'

'And why would you think that Mr Strong-and-Mighty?' her lips pressed together in a smile, but fury radiated from her eyes.

'I'm not trying to lie to you.'

'Not "trying"? Oh, so it comes naturally then?'

'That's not what I meant!' Samson said, feeling his anger rise.

'You know, I took a big risk with you. I've never opened up to a Hebrew before. I thought we were making something special—'

'We are!'

'No! Don't say that. You surprise me by proposing marriage. Then you raise my trust levels, only to smash them down again. Not once, not twice, but three times you've lied to me. How's a girl supposed to stay in a relationship like this? How could I marry a man who's so dishonest?'

Samson & the Siren

Samson knew she wasn't unreasonable, yet he also knew he couldn't tell her the truth. 'Look, it's not personal, OK.'

'Not personal? The man I love is lying to me, and it's not personal?'

Samson grinned. 'I love you too, let's eat!' he said with a wink—resorting to jokes as a coping mechanism.

'Ah, men!'

'Look, babe, there's just some things I need to keep secret, alright?' he said and shrugged his soldiers.

'Even from the woman you want to be your wife?'

Samson thought for a moment. He'd had an idea recently and, though it wasn't exactly a lie, it wasn't fully honest either. He didn't want to mislead the woman he loved, but he didn't want to lose her either—even if the relationship had become more emotionally taxing as of late.

'Well?' she asked. 'How can you keep this big secret from me, huh?'

He decided to go for it. He stared at her intensely. 'It's you I must keep the secret from most of all.'

Delilah shot him a look of disbelief. 'Wait, what? From me most of all? How does that work?'

'If you knew the secret, you'd be at risk. Many Philistines will already see you as a traitor just for marrying me. But, if my enemies knew that you knew the secret of my strength, they'd

The Oliver Anderson Trilogy

try to capture you—they'd torture you to get that information. I can't let that happen to you. I must protect those I love—that's why I tell no one.'

Delilah paused. His reason for keeping his secret made sense, but it didn't feel quite right. 'Why haven't you said this before?' she asked.

The real reason was that he hadn't thought of it until a few days ago. It wasn't exactly a lie. After all, knowing his secret *could* potentially put Delilah at greater risk.

'Because I didn't want you to be afraid. Yes, you'll have enemies because you're my wife. But I'm able to protect what's mine. Leave the secret with me and allow me to keep you safe. Delilah, give yourself to me in trust, and no harm will come to you.'

When he said those words, something unexpected happened. The possibility of running off with Samson flashed before Delilah's mind. In an instant, she saw what life, as Samson's wife, would be like—that he'd love and protect her. He'd take her from Philistia and the pain she'd know. For a second, a new life vision with a new community and a new God opened up. Until now, she'd never considered Samson a real partner. It had all been an act. But now, a moment of hesitation swept over her. *What if the love he's offering me is worth it? What if, instead of a better life in my current world, I need to enter a*

204

whole new world? What if Samson and Israel can give me something I can't find in Philistia? That vision of a new life was both a moment and an eternity. It was a second, yet in that second, she saw the possibility of her life going in a whole new direction—and her becoming a new person. She saw a picture of her, Samson, and their children. And in it, she was happy.

But after entertaining this consideration for a moment, contempt came crashing down upon it. *He's a Hebrew hillbilly. More financially well off than most, but nothing like elite Philistine society.* She dismissed her thoughts of a life in Israel with Samson as folly. Wherever that vision had come from, it was a door she must close and not consider again.

She also knew she must switch tactics if she was to get Samson's secret. Fortunately, her backup plan was ready, and she quickly rehearsed it in her mind.

Samson saw her thinking, but the content of those thoughts was a mystery to him. 'Look, I understand you're upset, but please understand.' Then, to his pleasant surprise, Delilah looked at him with smiling eyes, walked over to him, and melted in his arms. She laid her head against his chest, her hair, pressing up into his beard.

'Thank you,' she whispered. 'I understand now. You were just looking out for me.'

The Oliver Anderson Trilogy

Samson held her tight. 'Now, this is the girl that I love. I hate it when we fight.'

'Me too. Let me get some food. I have some leftover lamb from this morning. Let's eat, enjoy some wine in each other's arms—dream about our future together.'

'And will we be getting naked at the end of all this?'

'I dunno. What do you think?'

'Only if you're lucky,' Samson said smugly.

'Ha!'

'Well, you're gonna have to treat me right after that cold shoulder you gave me when I arrived.'

Delilah winked. 'I promise I'll make up for it.'

'I suppose it won't hurt to let you try,' Samson said with a smile.

'I'll do my best to soothe your emotions, princess,' Delilah said, 'Get cosy on the sofa. I'll come back with the lamb and wine.'

'Yes, ma'am.'

Samson & the Siren

33

DELILAH WATCHED HER victim stumble up the stairs and towards her bedroom. It worked.

She called softly to a servant-soldier from the next room. 'Deliver a message to the general. Tell him that we have Samson and that we need him here at once.'

'Are you sure, my lady? The other times he misled us. I wouldn't want to call the general unless—'

'This time is different,' she interrupted. 'Tell the general I used the tool he gave me. Tell him that his prisoner is ready.'

'As you wish, my lady,' the soldier said and turned with haste.

Delilah walked into the kitchen and examined the various knives. Finally, she slid one underneath her belt. 'This will do,' she said to herself. 'But first, I need to send him into a deep sleep.'

The Oliver Anderson Trilogy

Delilah knew that in his present condition, getting him to sleep would be easier than usual. The drugs, the alcohol, and the coming sex should all work together to put him into a deep enough sleep for her knife to do its magic.

***

Samson groaned face down on the bed. He heard heavy footsteps. It was as if a crowd had just arrived in the next room—but he was too groggy to wake himself and inspect.

'Hey, baby,' he mumbled. 'Are the servants working in the next room? Couldn't they wait till morning?' But there was no response.

'Delilah?' He swung his arm around on the bed, expecting to pat her naked body. 'Baby?' But there was no response. He noticed his head felt unusually cold. His mind began to crawl out of its fog and into the world of the awake. That's when he heard the cry.

'Samson! The Philistine soldiers are here!'

He knew that cry. He began to push his heavy body up. Where had he heard that cry before? That's right: Delilah. *She'd said that before. But why?* He couldn't quite remember. Had the soldiers attacked him here? *No, not here. What was it then? Oh, yes, that's right. It was a test.* Every time he'd shared one of his made-up secrets about his strength, she'd tested him on it. *But... I didn't tell her anything last night, did I?*

208

His mind spun with questions as he stood up on the bed, naked, and opened his eyes. The door flung open, and light from torches poured into the room.

'Samson! The Philistine soldiers are upon you!' Delilah's voice cried out again.

Now he was awake. Soldiers with torches were still filling the room. *This is really happening!* He was angry that soldiers would invade this space where he shared his love with the woman who'd soon be his wife. He harnessed that anger and let it fuel his jump off the bed and into the midst of soldiers. 'Die!' he screamed as he descended upon them. Somewhere, in the back of his mind, he wondered why his head was so cold.

He didn't know that he was bald—and that the Spirit of his God had left him.

***

Achish rested his hand on the shoulder of his most beautiful agent. The soldiers carried a bound and hooded Samson out of the door and into the night where a carriage awaited him that would immediately take him down to the prison in Gath. Achish was delighted. Now he needed to take his plan for Delilah to the next level.

He could feel her breathing was still heavy from the excitement. He reached over to rub her shoulder. 'You did it,' he said. 'I told you that you could.'

She looked at him, and her face lit up from the adrenaline pumping through her veins. 'Thank you! I did it, didn't I?'

'You are a hero.'

'Thanks. But without your help, I'd be leaving here a failure in the sight of the Lords.'

'OK, *we* did it. As a team: you and me. We've captured the man who was the greatest threat to our people's safety.'

'Yes, we did do it, didn't we?'

'The general and his top-secret agent.'

She smiled. 'I like the sound of that. I did do well, didn't I?' she asked again, eager to have him shower his fatherly affirmation on her.

'You were a star. The barbarian never saw it coming.'

'You should've seen our conversation last night. I was so subtle. I led him into conversations about his family and battles where he'd lost men. With the drug's help, he spilt his heart more than ever. By the time he started talking about no one ever cutting his hair, he didn't even realise what he was doing.'

Delilah's words rushed out as she explained how she'd done it. Achish smiled. She was like a school girl eager to tell a parent or teach how she'd won a race.

'You're a special girl, Delilah,' he said, stroking her cheek, 'You have a bright future in front of you. It's been an honour to help you achieve a success that will secure respect from the top

Samson & the Siren

levels of government. I'm ever so proud of you,' he said with as much sincerity as his voice and eye were able to reflect.

Achish's words tingled down her spine. The whole evening lifted her into a sense of euphoria that she hadn't felt since she was little. One of the most powerful men in the nation was praising her, not for her performance in bed but for a successful act of espionage that would save Philistine lives. The general's past abuses were too inconvenient for her to remember at that moment. It was enough that a strong and older man was proud of her.

'What will you do now?' Achish asked.

'After I calm down, I'll try to get some sleep. I want to pack up my things tomorrow morning and leave by noon. If I can be in Ekron by nightfall, I'd love to surprise my brother.'

Achish nodded. 'That sounds wonderful.'

'And you?'

'First, I'm headed back to the garrison with the soldiers—where we'll have a few drinks in light of our success. Then, once I've finished there, I'll head down to Gath to oversee Samson's interrogation.'

Still high on the intensity of the moment, she reached out and squeezed his arm. 'Will I see you again any time soon?' she asked. No sooner had she done so than she pulled back her hand. She realised, even in her excitement, that she was too forward. A sudden doubt about his trustworthiness flashed through her mind. 'I'm sorry. What I meant to ask was—'

'Don't worry about it,' Achish said, cutting her off. He had seen her open up and, try as she might to take it back, she'd already shown her newly developed feelings. 'You and I just won a major victory. Naturally, we'd want to celebrate together. I'm sure this event will ensure that we're always friends.'

'Friends? Yes, of course, friends and coworkers,' she said.

'Coworkers? Are you in the mood for more espionage?'

'No!' Delilah said and laughed. 'That's not what I meant. Actually, I'm not sure what I meant. I'm exhausted.'

'Then let me leave you well,' Achish said and leaned in to kiss her forehead. This time, he let his lip linger longer on her skin than before.

Delilah did nothing to push him away. 'Good-bye for now, then?'

'Don't worry. I'm sure our paths will cross again soon enough.' Achish said. He knew they would. He'd set things in motion that would ensure she'd be coming to him soon.

Samson & the Siren

34

'I'VE DECIDED WHAT to do.'

The two men looked over at Elise. 'Whaddya mean, darlin'?' William asked.

'Samson lost his strength and got captured because he compromised. He went against what he knew to be true and good. I can't let myself do that just because I don't wish to upset some teachers—and possibly my fellow students.'

'So what'll you do?' Oliver asked.

'I'll write an email to Ms O'Donnell today saying I can't go along with this. The school may have adopted those ideas—either out of sincere conviction or out of social pressure, who knows?—but I have not adopted them. So if they want to show my film, they must show it as it is. My film is trying to communicate a message, and I won't let them force me to say something I don't believe. For me, that would be lying.'

The Oliver Anderson Trilogy

There was silence in the room as both men looked admiringly at Elise. Then, finally, Oliver leaned over and kissed her on the cheek. 'I'm proud of you,' he said.

'Aye, I am too,' William added.

'Thanks, grandpa,' Elise said with a smile. 'But I don't think I'll be organizing a hunger strike.'

'Shame. Ye don't know how much fun yer missin' out on.'

Oliver laughed. 'We'll have to take your word for it, grandpa.'

'Any advice before I write it?' Elise asked.

'Be yer fabulous, gentle self. Sometimes people, Christians or otherwise, can become shrill when they're standin' up to injustice. Don't develop an edge when dealin' with those who support MAGBT. Be humble and gentle. Let people know yer not lookin' for a fight. Ye want the freedom to follow yer conscience just like you give them the freedom to follow theirs. Smile at 'em—and mean it.'

Elise stood up from her chair, walked over to William's bed, threw her arms around him and hugged him the best she could. He placed a hand on her head. 'Well, that's an unexpected treat,' he said.

'Thank you,' Elise replied. 'Oliver told me how wonderful you were, but today I've experienced it for myself.'

214

'Well, I'll be,' he said with a big smile. 'I oughta have a heart attack more often if it means gettin' this kinda love.'

'I think she appreciates your advice more than your heart attack, grandpa,' Oliver said.

'Probably right, lad.'

Elise lifted her head off his shoulder. 'Thank you. I appreciate how you didn't just tell me what to do when we first brought the issue up. You told me a story and allowed me to form my own thoughts.'

William bowed his head. 'Ye honour me, my lady,' he said.

'Oliver!'

'Yes?'

'Quick, go downstairs and buy somethin'.'

'Sure, grandpa. What do you need?'

'A ring.'

'A ring?'

'Yes, a ring, ye goin' deaf?'

'Well, I—'

'I need ye to hurry up and get engaged to this girl before ye do anythin' stupid enough to scare her off.'

'Oh.'

'I mean it. This lassie is gonna be the mother of my great-grandchildren.'

The Oliver Anderson Trilogy

Elise blushed. 'Thank you for your confidence in me, grandpa. But no need to pressure Oliver just yet. We need to graduate first, right Oliver?'

Oliver shook his head, clearly uncomfortable with the discussion. 'Yeah, sure. You two decide when I should pop the question, and I'll make a note of it.'

'Sorry lad,' William said. 'I guess we're givin' ye a hard time.'

'Now would be a good time for you to get back to the story.'

'Ok, then. Where was I? Oh, yes. So, After robbin' Samson of his strength, Delilah headed south to Ekron. But she'd soon find out that things weren't as expected.'

35

THE SUN WAS setting as the five donkeys approached Ekron. When they reached the gates, Delilah turned to the two male and two female servants who had accompanied her on the journey and thanked them for ensuring her safety. She had come to know all four throughout her seven months in the Sorek—the women especially—and valued their company and help.

After exchanging good-byes, Delilah dismounted her beast, held its reins, and headed into the small city towards her brother's apartment. It had been three months since her previous visit.

As she strolled down the streets, the smells and sounds of the city wrapped around her like a blanket. As much as she loved being in the Sorek, she missed the energy and creativity of the city. She'd missed the availability of foods brought in from the Aegean, the musicians, and the craftsmen. She'd only visited Ekron a few times in her life, but she liked it. The city wasn't as overwhelming as Gath, but it still had all the amenities and social life that one couldn't get in the countryside.

As she strolled along, she wondered if this could be home for her next season of life. She had enough money to live on for over a year—maybe two. She imagined buying a larger house where both she and Goliath could live together as a family. Though she knew she could prosper financially as a sex worker, she had no desire to return to that life anytime soon—certainly not in a small city like Ekron and not around her little brother. He'd hate that. *At the very least, I need a break from that. .*

Perhaps she could find another trade, or, maybe, she might find a man she'd look up to and marry. At twenty-one, she'd be older than the typical Philistine bride, but she knew she had beauty on her side for at least a few more years.

Her imagination spun with ideas of what the future might hold as she entered her brother's neighbourhood. She turned a corner with her donkey and walked down the road towards his apartment. As she got near, however, her musings on the future were cut abruptly short.

Soldiers?

Outside of her brother's house were two soldiers as if on sentry duty. She paused for a moment and looked around to make sure she was on the right street. Yes, she was sure of it. She held tight to her donkey and approached the young men.

'Excuse me, are you friends of my brother?' she asked.

The soldiers looked at each other. 'Um, I'm not sure,' one replied. 'Who's your brother?'

'The young man, who lives here. You're standing in front of his door.'

'You're the sister of the accused?'

The word hit her like a punch to the throat. 'A-accused?'

'Yes, Goliath, I believe his name is.'

Delilah shook her head in disbelief. 'No, that cannot be. You see, my brother oversees prisoners. He's a warden—an assistant warden. So there's no way he can be a criminal.'

The soldiers looked at each other again and shrugged. 'I'm sorry. A group of soldiers arrested him about three hours ago. They took him in.'

'Arrested?' Delilah asked in disbelief. 'But why?'

'We're not sure of the details. Why don't you go to the prison and ask? Do you know where it is?

'Yes, on the west side of town.'

'Correct. Your brother is being kept there for now. That's probably where you'll find your answers.'

The Oliver Anderson Trilogy

Delilah shook her head in disbelief, grabbed the donkey's reins and then turned and dragged her beast as she could towards the prison.

36

THE NEXT SEVENTY-TWO hours were a nightmarish whirlwind for Delilah. When she arrived at the Ekron jail, her brother wasn't there—they'd already taken him to Gath for sentencing. All she learned from the warden was that the authorities had found him selling illegal items on the black market—though he seemed hesitant to divulge any of the details.

It was late, and Delilah knew it was risky to travel at night—especially as a woman alone. She rented a room, but her anxiety didn't allow her to sleep. After a bite to eat in the morning, she remounted her donkey and began her journey to Gath.

The journey was only five hours, but it might as well have been five days. Delilah's fatigue and panic robbed her of all sense of time. The anxiety she had for her brother shattered the sense of hope and optimism she'd had about the future the day before. The only hope she dared to entertain was that these charges were a misunderstanding.

Delilah arrived mid-afternoon. It had been seven months since she'd left this city for the calm of Sorek. But now was not the time to revisit friends or her favourite shops. Instead, she made her way directly to the prison—a much larger one than what they had in Ekron.

It took Delilah nearly an hour to find someone willing to explain what was going on. After much pleading, some flirting, and no small bit of bribing, Delilah finally got to speak with the Gath warden himself. He was blunter than the warden at Ekron had been. He told her Goliath's situation directly: the authorities had charged him with conspiring with Egyptian forces to undermine the integrity of Philistia. The punishment for this treason would be death—with the plan being to execute him next week.

That's when she collapsed.

***

When Delilah awoke, she found herself curled up against a stone wall outside the prison. Then the bad news flooded back. Fear seized her. She'd always looked out for her little brother, but now she was helpless. Then, in her desperate longing for a solution, one name flashed across her mind: *Achish.*

Samson & the Siren

She ran back inside. *Somebody at the prison must know how to get a message to the General of National Safety.* She didn't have to look long.

'Sir, how can I get an emergency message to General Achish? He knows me. We've done work together.'

The elderly guard guessed by her appearance that she was wealthy and might be someone of importance. 'You're in luck. The general arrives here this evening.'

'He's coming here? Tonight?'

'Yes, we received an important prisoner yesterday, and General Achish will be overseeing his interrogation.'

Samson! In her concern for her brother, she'd forgotten all about him. *Yes, of course, he said he was coming down here.* There was simply too much happening to keep it all straight.

'Shall I have a message given to the general on your behalf?' the guard asked.

Delilah pulled two silver coins from her belt. 'Here, please make sure he gets the message as soon as he arrives.'

The guard's eyes widened. Two silver coins were as much as he made in a week. 'As you wish!'

'I wish to wait here until he arrives. Do you have a room where I can wait alone and rest?'

The guard squeezed the two silver coins in his hand. 'Follow me.'

The Oliver Anderson Trilogy

37

THE GENERAL ENTERED carrying a basket which he placed in the corner of the small room. His entrance disturbed the sleep of the one who'd been waiting for him.

Delilah opened her eyes. 'Achish?' The moment she recognized him, she stood up and flew across the floor. She'd waited for several hours—most of which she'd slept through. She threw her arms around him and buried her face in his beard. 'Thank you for coming to see me. I need your help. My brother—'

'I know,' he said, caressing her head. 'I got your message and went straight to the warden. He gave me a full report.'

She leaned back and looked pleadingly into his face. 'Please, Achish. My brother—he's a good boy. Whatever foolish thing he may have done, it certainly isn't worthy of death.'

Achish took her hands in his and spoke softly to her. 'I believe you, Delilah. Truly. But it doesn't look good for Goliath.'

'But why?'

'He was a soldier in service to Philistia and was found to be using his wartime position to import and sell Egyptian products. His actions were contributing to the Egyptian economy. The authorities see it as a slap in the face to the soldiers who are still fighting down there.'

'B-but it was only a handful of rings, wasn't it?'

'How do you know? That evidence is supposed to be confidential.'

'He... he told me.'

Achish's face took on a look of shock. 'You mean you knew about this?'

Delilah's heart raced at the thought that she might be incriminating herself. 'I-I didn't know it was serious. Please don't—'

Achish raised his hand and gently covered her mouth with his fingers. 'Shhh. It's just us in this room. Don't tell anyone else what you just told me—it could land you in trouble as well. But your secret is safe with me.'

The Oliver Anderson Trilogy

Tears welled up in her eyes, and she squeezed Achish closer. 'Thank you. I'm so sorry, I told him to be careful, but I should've insisted he stop.'

He placed his hand back on top of her head. 'Come now, my dear. Don't blame yourself.'

'Please, can't you do something for my brother? Can't you make it go away? It was an honest mistake. I'll make sure he never does it again.'

'I'm afraid it's not that simple. Even I have to obey the law of the Philistine Lords and accept the consequences it demands. Only the Lords can issue a pardon forgiving a treasonous offence.'

'Is there nothing you can do, Achish? Won't one of the Lords listen to you? Can't you appeal his case? It'll destroy me if they execute him.'

Achish sighed. 'I'm sorry. Only aristocrats have the right to appeal their cases. Everyone else must accept the consequences the first time around. I cannot change Philistine jurisprudence.'

Delilah's arms fell to her side, and she walked towards the wall in despair. 'There was a day when my family were aristocrats. It's been more than ten years since we lost that.'

'I'm so sorry, my dear. I wish there were something I could do. I can, at the very least, arrange for you to see your brother

Samson & the Siren

before his execution. Also, I own several houses in this city. One of them is currently free—use it for as long as you need it.'

Delilah turned from the wall and looked at him. 'Thank you. I don't know what I'd do without you. I'd like very much to see my brother now, but I-I don't know if I could handle it emotionally.'

Achish walked over to her and took her hand. 'Let's sit,' he said gently. 'I'll do everything I can to help you.'

'If I lose him, Achish, I don't know what I'd do.'

'You are a strong woman. You'll make it.'

'No, don't you see, I can't just resign myself to this fate. I'd do anything to save him.'

'Anything?'

'Yes, I'd lay down my life for my little brother.'

'Well, there is one way,' he said and looked down as if to say something difficult. 'But it's probably not worth mentioning.'

'What?'

'No, it's a long shot and one you'd reject immediately. I only mean there is something within the realm of possibility.'

Her eyes lit up. 'Tell me!'

'I hesitate even to say it. It is too much.'

She grabbed his arm. 'Please!'

'I know it's something that would be abhorrent to you.'

'No, Achish, I'd do anything to help him. Really!'

'Well,' he said and cleared his throat, 'The one way you could appeal his case to the Lords is if you were an aristocrat.'

Delilah looked at him, puzzled. 'You already said that. You know we're no longer aristocrats,' she said with no tone of accusation.

Achish took a deep breath. 'Yes. But you could become one.'

'Huh?'

'If you were to become an aristocrat before his execution, that status would pass to your immediate family—in this case, your brother.'

'You're speaking in riddles. How could I possibly become an aristocrat again—and in less than a week?'

'There is a way, but I fear even to say it.'

'How?'

'It'll sound crazy.'

'Achish, if there's even a chance, I need to hear it—no matter how ridiculous.'

Achish stared straight at her. 'If you marry an aristocrat, you, as the wife of an aristocrat, would become an aristocrat.'

The thought was a slap across her face. 'Marriage? What? Who? There's no way I could get an aristocrat to marry me in less than a week. I had a couple of clients that were aristocrats, but I haven't spoken to them in seven months—they've probably found new mistresses or whores by now.'

Samson & the Siren

'Perhaps if you contacted them?'

She thought for a second. 'No. If there were even a fraction of chance, I'd try it. But there isn't. None of the aristocrats I knew would consider making me one of their legitimate wives or having heirs with me. It was only ever about the sex and stroking their middle-aged egos.'

'You can't think of anyone?'

Delilah buried her face in her hands and sobbed. 'No... there's no one.'

Achish laid his hand on her shoulder. 'There is one option, though it may seem like the worst of times to bring up such a matter.'

Delilah looked up at him. 'Yes?'

Achish smiled tenderly. 'Over the last seven months of working together, well, I've become very fond of you, Delilah. You're a special girl. Truly, I know no one like you. And I, well, I'm an aristocrat—though perhaps in your grief you've forgotten.'

The penny dropped. Delilah suddenly realised what he was getting at. She opened her mouth to speak.

'Wait, please,' Achish said. 'Just let me finish. I know you might not feel about me what I feel for you, but if you would consider, it would be my great joy and honour if you were to marry me.'

229

'Marry you?' a title wave of emotion swept over her. 'But…
Can you? How many wives do you have?'

'I have two wives at present,' he said. 'And, as you probably
know, an aristocrat can have up to four.

'Yes, I know,' she said, staring at him in a storm of confused
emotion. She didn't know what she felt towards Achish
anymore. 'Would… would you do that for me?'

Achish nodded. 'With joy.'

Delilah thought it through. She knew it would take her
some time to sort out her feelings for Achish. But it wasn't
about that—not now. She might decide later that she loved
him—and something within her enjoyed his strong presence.
But that's not what would determine this. At this moment, all
that mattered was that her brother needed her and that he
would die if she didn't.

'Yes,' she said.

'Yes?'

'Yes, I'll marry you.'

'You understand,' Achish said slowly, 'I don't want to force
you.'

'I know. I feel your affection for me. You've looked out for
me as a friend and a father. I wish I could pledge to you my
heart, but, at the moment and under these circumstances, I can

Samson & the Siren

only pledge my faithfulness as your wife. You can have me. Just, please, save my brother.'

'Then we will marry tomorrow morning. I'll petition Goliath's case immediately after.'

The thought of marrying so quickly was overwhelming, but she didn't want to delay seeking her brother's release. 'OK. Let's do it.'

Achish took her hand and stood, raising with him. 'Let's move fast. We need to save Goliath. I'll have one of my servants take you back to my house here in the city. It's not one where either of my wives or anyone else lives other than two servants who will attend to you. You will get warm food and, if you desire one, a bath. Make yourself comfortable.'

'When will I see you?'

'I have some business I must attend to first. While I do that, just relax. I'll join you before it gets too late,' the general said. He leaned in and kissed her—this time on the lips. 'Tonight, we'll share a bed.'

That thought gave her pause. 'Of course,' she said, feeling a strange mixture of desire and fear that she didn't quite understand. 'Tonight we bed. Tomorrow we marry. Then, as an aristocrat couple—'

'As a couple, we save your brother.'

She looked into his eye. 'Thank you, Achish. You've saved me.'

***

Achish watched her walk down the street from the entrance to the prison. A small laugh escaped him. He no longer had to hide his amusement. He'd almost forgotten it was a performance and, for a little while, thought that perhaps he really was her saviour and guardian. She seemed to feel more indebted to him than he'd dreamed possible. She would soon be his trophy—a tribute to his powers of manipulation. *Well played, Achish. Tonight you'll enjoy the fruit of your labours.*

He needed to send a generous gift to the warden in Ekron. If it weren't for his diligent spycraft in the comings and goings of her brother, this wouldn't have been possible. But that could wait. There was someone he needed to see—someone waiting for him in the most secure cell in the building.

Samson.

He picked up his basket and headed down the hall.

38

'SO, THE LAW has caught up with our infamous rebel,' the general said as he walked into the cell, carrying his basket.

Samson looked up. He was sitting on the floor, bound with ropes between two guards. 'Achish! Wow, the big guns are here. It's been a while, hasn't it? How's the eye?'

'It's "General" to you,' Achish said, placing the basket on the floor. 'I hope the new accommodations are to your liking.'

'Let's see: damp, smelly, crawling with insects, stinks. Yes, I'd say it's Philistine décor at its finest. I'm only disappointed you haven't greeted me with a kiss.'

The general pressed his lips and smiled. 'Hm. Even now, you're defiant. Remarkable.'

'Know what they say: old habits die slowly.'

The Oliver Anderson Trilogy

'As will you.'

'Good, I hate it when people rush things. Few people take pride in their work anymore.'

'I see you've acquired some bruises,' Achish said, ignoring his retort. 'I hope the soldiers weren't unnecessarily rough.'

'Gentle as maids.'

'And yet, this time you didn't get away?'

Samson smiled. 'And miss out on all this? Never!'

'Only our best for the Hebrew champion. Are the ropes too tight?'

'Well, if you'd come over and loosen them, we could have a little cuddle.'

'Another time, perhaps. Anyway, you've had lots of cuddles lately, haven't you?'

Samson took a deep breath. 'Look, what's she—'

'Fool!' the general interrupted. 'You're not the first man to have his downfall at the hands of a woman. Though, I confess, I've never enjoyed watching it happen this much.'

Samson opened his mouth, but words were slow to come out. The general knew he'd touched a sore spot. He laughed. 'Struggling for words? You don't think she ever cared for you, do you?' Samson bit his lip. It had only been less than

Samson & the Siren

two days, and his soul was still processing the betrayal. 'Well? No words?'

'I think you're jealous, big guy,' shot back.

The general scowled. 'Jealous? What could a Philistine general ever envy in a Hebrew dog.'

'Because I had her.'

'You had nothing! She played you—she only pretended to care for you, and you bought it like cheap wine. In any case, tonight, she'll be in my bed, giving herself to me willingly, while you play with yourself in here.'

Samson stared at the floor in front of him. He knew it was his foolishness that had led to this embarrassment—and he hated that the general was his mocker. 'What can I say, General? You two deserve each other.'

'We'll laugh at your expense before making love.'

'Well, you know what they say about sloppy seconds.'

No one in Philistia ever spoke to General Achish with such flippancy. 'Shut up! You'll be our slave and suffer for your defiance.'

'Did you say "shut-up" to me?' Samson said as if insulted by a child. 'Listen, Achish, why don't you come back later when you're ready to have an adult conversation?'

'Hebrew filth!'

The Oliver Anderson Trilogy

'You're losing your cherished cool, Achish. You need to sit down and calm—'

'It's General and, no, I'll stand. You're weak as any man now. Your magic no longer works. You cannot back up your cavalier words with might.'

'I'll admit, I've had better days.'

'Ah, but they will only be getting worse, you see.'

'Promises, promises. Philistines aren't great at keeping them.'

The general walked over and placed his hand on Samson's bald head. 'Do you like your new haircut?' he said. Samsom turned his head and faced the wall—another sore spot. 'Nothing clever to say about that? Do you think your hair is the only thing we'll be taking?'

'Well, I could shed a few pounds. Unfortunately, all the crappy Philistine food your whore cooked for me has added some weight.'

'Your words will cost you, Samson.'

'I'm afraid I left my money belt at home.'

'We won't kill you. Not now. It will be far more satisfying to watch you waste away your days as a slave in this prison. Also, I was thinking of a personal payment—in response to something you once took from me.'

Samson & the Siren

A shiver shot down Samson's back. He guessed what the general was implying. 'Ah, crap,' he said and blinked hard.

'Yes, you guess correctly.'

'Make it the left one?'

'Oh, I'll be taking payment with interest. But, first, I have a present for you,' the general said as he reached down and picked up his basket. Samson was silent. 'You see, I figured that if we were to take your sight, at least we could give you something in return. So I wanted to bless you with something to look at before we performed our delicate operation—a last memory before the lights go out,' Achish said as he reached into the basket, grabbed what was inside, and set it on the floor right before Samson.

Samson yelled. His arms and legs thrashed wildly against the chains as he fought to get free. He'd seen a decapitated human head before, but he didn't expect to see this one.

It was Malachi.

Samson spat at him. 'You bastard! You killed an old man.'

Achish laughed. 'You want to know something? He begged for his life before we cut him. He pleaded, like a dog.'

'Liar! I'll kill you before this is over. Your head for his!'

'All evidence to the contrary,' Achish said with a smirk. 'Guards! Get the pokers. Both eyes—and do it slowly.'

The Oliver Anderson Trilogy

39

IT WAS GOLIATH'S seventh day delivering food in the Gath prison. His tasks were thankless and straightforward compared to the role he had at Ekron. But he wasn't complaining. After all, two weeks earlier, he'd been facing a death sentence. A demotion to a menial job may be unfortunate, but it's not as bad as being demoted to the grave. Still, though he was grateful to his sister for pulling strings to keep him alive, he hated the system that had caused these circumstances. *I fight for Philistia, and this is the thanks I get. They were just rings!*

The prison was massive compared to the one in Ekron. There were eighty-three prisoners here. Most of them were locked up together in larger rooms. A few of them, however, were locked up by themselves in smaller ones.

Samson & the Siren

Goliath was curious about the prisoner at the east end of the building. He was given a private room plus two extra soldiers—in addition to the regular guards. Every day he'd give the food tray to one of the soldiers, who then brought it into the prisoner.

Today the soldiers were gone. The powers that be no longer considered the prisoner an escape risk. Goliath had heard that this prisoner was a high-value Hebrew militia leader and a fearsome fighter. The soldiers, he further heard, had blinded him and assigned him to grind the prison's grain.

Goliath set the tray down on the ground and removed the keys from his pocket. Usually, he could do this one-handed, but the solitary rooms had two locks with two different keys. He inserted them into the door and turned both simultaneously. *Click, clack.* The door opened. He lifted the tray and walked in.

The first thing he noticed was that the room was larger than the other solitary cells. *Perhaps so the visitors might be allowed or... soldiers with interrogation equipment.* The second thing Goliath noticed was the prisoner. He sat in the room's corner with iron chains clasping his wrists and ankles. His body leaned forward, pointing his bald head right at Goliath. *Is this the guy who killed hundreds of our soldiers? He doesn't look so impressive,* he thought as he set the food in front of the captive.

239

His hand grabbed the wooden baton at his side. 'Prisoner!' he called. 'Wake up. You have an hour to eat your meal. After that, I'll be back to collect.'

Samson spoke but didn't move. 'A full hour to eat? You must've brought me a feast. I hope you didn't burn the goat—I'm not fond of it when it's too dry. Make sure there's a nice fig cake to finish it off. I'm partial to those.'

'Very funny, Hebrew. It's some bread and a hunk of cheese.'

'That's it? My view of Philistine hospitality has somewhat lessened of late.'

'From what I've heard,' Goliath said, 'your view of everything has lessened of late.'

'Ha, well, yes. Painfully true,' Samson said and reached his hand out to find the tray. Goliath turned to leave when Samson asked, 'Are you new here? I haven't heard your voice before.'

Goliath stopped and looked over his shoulder. 'It's my first day serving you because the soldiers have given you food till now.'

'You don't sound like a food delivery boy. You speak with confidence.'

'I was a soldier before. But what's it to you?'

'"Was"? A man doesn't go from soldier to a job like this unless someone demoted him.'

Samson & the Siren

'Worry about your own problems! I doubt you'll be getting out of here any time soon—unless it's to go downstairs to grind more grain.'

Samson chuckled. 'OK—calm down. I'm not trying to pry. And, yes, it's been a hard couple of weeks for me. But I could be dead. To be alive is a gift.'

'A gift? Look at yourself. Most men would prefer death.'

'The time of my death is in God's hands. Whatever time I have left, I receive it gratefully. Heaven knows I wasted enough of it when I was free.'

'So you regret fighting against us?'

'Do I regret my militia work? No. The Philistines abused us and stole our freedom. But I regret a lot of other things—some of which resulted in the death of a good friend,' Samson said and paused for a moment. 'What's your name, by the way?'

'Goliath,' he said. 'I suppose if I am the one bringing you food each day, you should at least know it. But don't expect me to be kind to anyone who's taken up arms against Philistia.'

'I expect nothing.'

'You shouldn't.'

'It's freeing, really,' Samson said.

'You may be a lot of things right now, but free isn't one of them.'

241

'Once you stop thinking you deserve so much, you're free to be grateful and enjoy what you have.'

Goliath shook his head. 'Are you supposed to be a militia fighter or a sage?'

'Locked up in here, I have little else to do but to reflect on my misadventures.'

'You wanna talk about misadventures? My life got screwed because of a few rings I picked up in Egypt and tried to sell.'

'Ah, the embargo against Egyptian goods,' Samson remarked. 'Is that still a law they enforce?'

'Yeah, I thought it was merely one on the books too.'

'Well, I'm just a Hebrew prisoner, but it sounds harsh if you care for my opinion. I thought you guys were trying to make peace with Egypt so that you could focus on us Hebrews.'

'Exactly! They even tried to execute me for this! They would've done so had not my sister, Dee, intervened. Thanks to her, I now only have five years of service in this prison.'

'How'd she pull that off?'

'She married an aristocrat—a general at that. That qualified me, as her family, for an appeal.'

'I'm being served food by the brother of an aristocrat lady? What service! I'll be sure to leave a big tip on the way out.'

Samson & the Siren

'Shut up, Moron,' Goliath said with a grin—beginning to feel entertained by the strange prisoner. 'And, so you know, that makes me, as her sibling, an aristocrat too.'

'An aristocrat serving prisoners?'

'Better than a death sentence.'

'Gotcha, kid. It looks like you're doomed to live after all.'

'Yeah, I suppose.'

'You grateful for what your sister did?'

'Well, yeah.'

'Then let's both give thanks to Heaven that our hearts are still beating and our heads still on our bodies.'

'You pray a lot then? My sister does too.'

'I haven't spent my life praying to God as I should.'

'Which one?' Goliath asked.

'Israel prays to just one: the Creator God of Heaven and earth.'

'A high-Creator God, huh? Yeah, here in Philistia, we have plenty for you to choose. Pick any god you like. We imported our gods from the Aegean and have added to them some Canaanite gods as well.'

'How do you know which one to pray to?'

'Whichever one we feel like.'

'Doesn't that make your feelings your god?' Samson asked.

'Perhaps. Is that so bad?'

The Oliver Anderson Trilogy

'I've spent too much of my life serving my feelings.'

'Sounds like you've got a story,' Goliath said.

'A story involving women, and one woman in particular. You married?'

'What, me? No, I'm only nineteen.'

'I was nineteen when I first married—to a Philistine gal if you're curious. And my last gal, well, I thought I was in love, but it seems she played me.'

'Ouch. Well, there's not much that could make me pity an enemy combatant, but woman trouble, that almost makes it possible. Was she a snake?'

'Definitely. But, still, it was my fault. I knew she wasn't the type of girl Heaven wanted me to have. My best friend, a servant, even tried to warn me—and he died because of it.'

'Women are the downfall of many men.'

'When we trust ourselves to their promises, yes. They're here today and gone tomorrow. Learn from my mistake. Whenever you're about to commit yourself to a woman, don't ask, "Do I love her?" Instead, ask, "Do I trust her?"'

'Sounds like the type of dating advice my sister, Dee, would give me.'

'Your big sister sounds like a wise woman. If you ever do marry, find someone like her.'

'I will… though maybe less bossy.'

Samson & the Siren

Samson gave a silent laugh. 'Well, let's both make the best out of the rest of our lives.'

'I only have to serve this five-year work sentence, and then I'm free again. What good could you possibly find in here?'

'As I said, I'm still alive. Heaven is humbling me, and I know now how much I need that.'

'Well, good luck,' Goliath said and then looked at the door. 'Go ahead and eat your food. I'll be back in an hour to collect the tray.'

Samson bowed his head, gave thanks, and began to eat.

40

SAMSON WAS THINKING. Other than grind grain and converse with his meal delivery boy, there was simply nothing else to do but to think.

And pray.

Occasionally, a guard would escort him outside where he might feel the warmth of the sun on his skin and enjoy the company of another enemy of the State. But these occurrences were few. As the months went by, it was Goliath alone with whom he ever shared any meaningful conversation. He regretted that he'd let his inner chaos keep him from fulfilling the divine call. But he was grateful that, failure though he was, a slow and gradual awareness of Heaven's nearness and goodness was reemerging.

He was not dead yet and, though he did not understand why God had kept him alive, he was learning to trust His providence. There was something yet for him to learn or to do—but what that might be, he had no idea. For now, his job was to be an ox.

Instead of an ox to grind the prison grain, they hitched Samson to the mill and told him to push or be whipped. At first, the job nearly destroyed him. He simply didn't have strength. But, as the weeks went by, his muscles grew in both his legs and upper body. It was tedious but not impossible.

Then there were his memories. As with many who become blind in the middle of their lives, Samson feared that he'd one day forget the world of images he once took for granted. He mentally reviewed colours, landscapes, and faces. Even if he escaped, he would never *see* his childhood home again. Then there was the last image he ever saw—Malachi. He knew the details of that image would be burned into his memory until the day he died—whether he wanted it there or not.

At times, the memory of his failures tempted him to despair. But he remembered the words of his mother, who'd taught him to give thanks always—so he'd spend whole afternoons finding reasons to be grateful. He even found something to be thankful for regarding his blindness: he'd never make the mistake of being seduced by a Philistine woman's beauty again. It was impossible. His eyes were a gift, but they'd gotten him into trouble. Throughout his life, he'd lusted after the beauty of

247

Philistine women. He'd thrown himself at these lovely ladies even when his reason knew better than to do so. His blindness ensured a pretty face would never deceive him again.

Not that he planned on meeting any women behind his prison bars. Still, God had kept him alive, and now he was praying more than ever before. He had an ever-growing faith that God still had something more for him.

Samson & the Siren

41

'JUST A LITTLE more lip paint,' Delilah said to herself as she placed the final stroke of red on her mouth. She stared into the reflecting glass as she finished applying her makeup. Her husband would be arriving soon to pick her up and take her to the celebration. It was harvest time, and Dagon needed his worship so that he'd send the latter rains.

Delilah had been the third wife of general Achish for nearly a year, and she was aware of the change. Not just a change in life circumstances—that was clear enough. But in her. Having not had the opportunity to observe her parents' relationship during her youth, she was never sure how marriage should work. But she hadn't imagined it would be like this.

It was hard for her to describe what it was, but Delilah was changing, and she knew it. Her vision, drive, and dreams were fading. Something was missing that was once there—a part of her that she struggled to remember. She vaguely remembered that she had been someone bold. But now, anxiety was her close companion. Sometimes just going outside made her nervous.

Her brother's visits were the joy for her existence. They worked him hard at the prison, but he could often get away for lunch and join her at her large but lonely house. They'd laugh and remember old times. They'd count down how many more years and months he had to go until his sentence was up when he could pursue a livelihood apart from his menial work with prisoners. Now that his family once again had aristocrat status, doors would open for him to thrive. He, at least, had a sense of vision—even if she lacked any for herself. Delilah knew he was alive because of her, and somehow that added an element of meaning into a life otherwise adrift without purpose.

As for Achish, she wasn't sure if she loved him. Perhaps she never had. But she *was* sure she needed him. She'd get ill if too much time passed between his visits to her house. Anxiety seized her at the very thought that he might one day discard her. He was the one who protected her and made everything alright.

Yes, he'd often neglect her or talk down to her and treat her like nothing more than an ornament to be worn on his arm at public events. She loathed that. And, yet, she couldn't imagine life any other way. Her life was a golden cage, and she'd forgotten what life was like on the outside. A part of her had died. She'd lost something along the way, but she wasn't sure what it was or where exactly she'd lost it.

***

'So, where are you taking me today? This isn't the way to the courtyard,' Samson said to Goliath and wrapped his arms around him as they rode on a horse through the city.

'Well, it's not to give you a tour of Gath.'

'Shame. My blind eyes were eager to see the sights.'

'It's a celebration,' Goliath replied. 'Before each harvest, Lords, aristocrats, and the whos-who in Gath gather at Dagon's temple to sacrifice and ask for his goodness.'

'Does he listen?'

The young man paused before answering. He'd become accustomed to meaningful conversations with this prisoner, and they weren't in the habit of giving each other trite answers. 'Maybe,' he said thoughtfully, 'some years are good, some years aren't.'

'How do you know Dagon is the right god, out of all of the Philistine gods, to pray to?'

'I suppose because our priests tell us so.'

'Why should Dagon, or any of your gods, listen to you and show you favour?'

'We sacrifice and pray to them. It might depend on their

mood,' Goliath said and paused. 'What about your god? How do you get him to do you a favour?'

'The God of Israel is not like the gods of Canaan or the ones from the Aegean. He's the Creator-God over Heaven and earth. He's not some temperamental adolescent and doesn't change his mind as men do. He has no equal.'

Goliath smiled. 'That's quite a description.'

'And, as for favours, no one can give to God that he should repay. If he were ever hungry, he wouldn't ask us for food. He gives to us because he has compassion.'

'Does he never get angry with you?'

'Oh, yes. Our God certainly does—whenever we ignore his laws or serve other gods. But he forgives the humble and those who turn from their arrogance and sin.'

'Nice,' Goliath said. 'Can't say Dagon has much of a reputation for forgiveness. You either please him, or you don't.'

'So where do I fit in in today's act of worship? Am I just gonna sit and listen, or do I need to grind Dagon's corn?'

'I wish I could tell you. The warden ordered me to bring you and then return you when it was over. You'll be part of the entertainment—I know that much. They see you as a trophy.'

'It feels good to be cherished.'

Goliath laughed. 'That's one way of looking at it. But, whatever they have in store, you should be prepared for some

Samson & the Siren

top tier mockery—and a bit of abuse.'

Samson sighed. 'Great,' he said. 'I think I'd rather be back in prison grinding grain.'

'I don't blame you. It might not be pleasant.'

'Still, my God has been good to me.'

'I wouldn't be thanking Dagon or any god if I were about to be spat on or made a fool of.'

'I thank my God because I'm alive and because he's forgiven my sins. I've had a lot of those.'

'How do you know He's forgiven your sins? Is it because you've been so good?'

Samson gave a silent laugh and said, 'No. Not because I'm good. It's because he's good.'

The Oliver Anderson Trilogy

42

DELILAH CLUNG TO his arm. She'd only been inside Dagon's temple twice before and never as an aristocrat. But now she had the good seats. She gazed at the countless thousands that had gathered to watch the sacrifice, join in the songs, and watch the entertainment. She felt the energy of their voices reverberating through the building. Her eyes followed the two stone pillars at the centre that ran up to the stone ceiling. Gath had some impressive buildings, but Dagon's temple was an architectural wonder. There was nothing among the Canaanites or Hebrews that came close to its magnificence. There was a time, not long ago, when she would've thrived on the energy of being amongst so many excited people. But, at the moment, it was overwhelming.

Elite couples introduced themselves, eager to meet Achish's beautiful young wife. She fought to keep their names straight and, even though she'd had aristocratic clients in her former days, she felt awkward and out of place here. Here, she was in a large group of both men and women—whereas before, she was used to manipulating a singular man in private. But there was something else. It wasn't just the people or her surroundings—*she* was different. Her ability to control and influence others was not what it had been.

'Have a seat, my dear,' Achish spoke into her ear above the noise of thousands of people chatting away. She obeyed his word, and they sat together in front of the area where the priests, singers, and entertainment would soon be appearing. 'Do you know what happens first?'

'No,' Delilah replied. 'What?'

'It's the same program every year,' Achish said, happily instructing his wife. 'The musicians will start with a couple of songs. Then, Dagon's chief priest will come out and say a few words. After that, the entertainment then more songs, and, finally, the sacrifice.'

Delilah liked it when her husband explained things clearly. She felt secure. 'Thank you for taking me here,' she said. She kissed him on the cheek and held tightly onto his arm once again.

The young singers and musicians came out to the centre of the arena, just behind the altar and before the columns. They wore no clothes, but colourful paints covered their bodies in honour of Dagon and the event. A hush came over the crowd, and the musicians began chanting and playing the instruments.

What Delilah noticed most of all were the drums. She'd never been so close to so many large drums before. The percussion moved through her, and, as the rhythm built, her body released its tension. Her mind wandered to pleasant places and was soon strolling through the vineyards and olive tree groves of the Sorek valley.

It took her a minute to descend from her fantasy back to the temple when the music ended and the priest began talking. She only became conscious of what he was saying towards the end of his announcements. She snapped back to attention when she heard him pronounce the word 'Sorek'.

'…a war trophy for your amusement. A leader of the Hebrew militia!'

She knew those words. It meant something, but it took her a moment to understand. When she saw the man the soldiers led to the centre of the arena, the penny dropped.

Her head snapped towards Achish. 'What's *he* doing here?'

Samson & the Siren

43

'SOUNDS NICE. CAN'T say we have anything quite like it back in Israel.'

'These are Aegean drums. They're three times bigger than you'd find in Canaan,' Goliath said.

'It is a joy to hear them—though I imagine they're singing to Dagon.'

'Singing about Dagon, to be precise.'

'Gotcha. When do I go on?'

'Soon. The entertainment will begin, and then the soldiers will parade you around the arena. Can't promise that you won't get some rotten egg thrown at you.'

'Hm, fun times,' Samson said. 'Can't blame them. If I were in their position, I'd probably do the same.'

The music died down. 'It looks like you're about to go on. Good luck!'

'Perhaps I can get my monthly bath early. I think I might need it after this.'

'Ha! Yes, you'll need that and a haircut. It's getting a bit hairy up on top.'

Samson ran his hand through his hair. 'Hm. It's grown. I—'

That's when he heard his name shouted by the priest and the roar of the crowd that followed. He was up. Two soldiers came and grabbed Samson, one on each arm.

'Have fun!' Goliath shouted as they forced Samson into the centre of the arena. Four men, covered in paint, approached Samson and began to dance around him. They spat, shouted, and slapped him on the face. The guards stood by on either side and laughed at the teasing.

For Samson, it was dizzying. He had no one or nothing to hold on to in his blindness and could only guess where they'd strike him next. With the roar of the crowd, his hearing couldn't help him get his bearings either. He took a deep breath and whispered, 'Help me bear my punishment.'

From the sidelines, Goliath watched the aggressive circus taking place in centre stage. At first, he was mildly amused. Though Samson had been respectful to him over the last year, he was still an enemy combatant. 'That'll teach him,' he muttered to himself as he watched Samson spin about under a shower of slaps from the painted jesters.

Samson & the Siren

At first, it looked like Samson might get through the day with nothing more than a few blows to his body and his pride. But then the soldiers got involved. One of them approached Samson from behind, his hand clothed in a gauntlet, and punched him on the back of the head. The blow was as disorienting as it was painful. Samson crashed onto the tiled floor. 'Our god has handed our enemy Samson to us!' the soldier shouted as the crowd cheered to Dagon.

A Philistine Lord stood on the front row and roared out, 'The gods have given us our enemy who destroyed our land and multiplied our dead!'

Samson rolled over in the dirt. The first conscious thought that flashed through his mind was that he might not leave Dagon's temple alive. 'Yahweh, help me,' he cried.

The soldier kicked Samson on the side. The other did likewise. Soon they were contesting to see who could kick him the hardest. The crowds cheered with rapturous delight. After their unsuccessful campaign in Egypt, seeing someone who personified the enemy beaten and mocked before them ignited the national pride. 'Kill him!' some screamed.

Goliath gritted his teeth. He hadn't expected them to go lightly on Samson, but watching a prisoner under his care beaten to this degree made him uncomfortable. Guards were not supposed to let other people kill their prisoners.

259

The wild cheers from the crowd intoxicated the soldiers. They were not used to being the centre of entertainment. One of them grabbed Samson by the arm and pulled him to his feet. Samson groaned and reached for his sides, his chest cut and bloody from the kicks. The first soldier pointed to the two pillars and shouted something to the second. He grinned. They marched Samson in between the two pillars and, with one holding his left hand and one his right, they swung him as hard as they could, facefirst, into the pillar. Samson's nose exploded with blood. But, no sooner had the pain from that blow registered that they swung him backwards into the other pillar. That blow, right on the back of the head, rendered him semi-unconscious. His feet gave way, and he became dead weight in the hands of the soldiers.

Goliath ran to the centre of the area. He knew his warden wouldn't be happy if a prisoner died under his watch. Samson might've been an enemy soldier, but he was an honourable one—and it offended whatever sense of right and wrong that Goliath had within him to see his prisoner die this way.

He bent down and placed his hand on his head. The soldiers took a step back. 'Samson, can you hear me?' he asked. There was no response. 'Samson!'

Finally, Samson coughed. 'Am I dead yet?'

Goliath smiled. 'If you're gonna get killed, don't do it on my

Samson & the Siren

watch. Are you trying to get me fired?'

Samson hurt too much to laugh. 'Sorry. It was careless of me to run into those walls like that.'

'They were pillars, actually.'

'Whatever they are,' he said and coughed again. 'I'll do better next time.'

Goliath stood up and turned to the soldiers. 'You've had your fun with him, but I need to retake custody. He's going back to the prison with me.'

The soldiers looked at each other. One, the bigger of the two, turned to Goliath. 'It ain't over till the priest says it's over. We're just gettin' warmed up.'

'I don't mind that you humiliate or rough him up. But I'm responsible for bringing him back *alive*,' Goliath said, trying to sound more confident than he felt speaking to the two bigger soldiers.

'Alright, boy,' one of them said. 'We won't kill him. We'll just come as close as we can.'

The other laughed. 'Yeah, don't worry ya pretty little head, me boy. The folks are lovin' this. Ya gotta lettem have fun.'

Goliath wasn't sure what to say. He knelt again next to Samson and spoke into his ear. 'I'm telling them they can't kill you. But I'm not sure I can stop them from making you wish you were dead.'

A look of dread contorted Samson's already bruised and bloody face. 'More fun, eh?'

'Shut yer Hebrew face, ya dog,' the bigger soldier said, standing right above them. 'We're gonna beat ya, then we're gonna beat ya some more—just like we're gonna beat all Israel.'

Samson tried to spit in what he imagined was the direction of the soldier's voice, but the saliva just drooled out from between his busted lips. He turned on his side and used his elbow to begin pushing himself up. 'You're not touching Israel,' Samson gasped as he raised to his knees.

The first soldier laughed. 'Hey, look here, I think he's ready for some more. He thinks them Hebrews gonna stop us.'

Samson stumbled onto his feet. He reached out his hand and found Goliath's shoulder to balance his broken body.

The soldiers laughed again and walked towards the crowd. 'Do yas wanna see some more?' he shouted. The crowd roared again. 'Do yas wanna see us whip him like we're gonna whip those little filthy Hebrews?'

The crowd stood on their feet and cheered. 'Kill Samson! Kill the Hebrews!'

Anger shot up Samson's spine, and he felt the strength of fury begin to burn. It was one thing for them to mock him—he'd earned that. It was another for them to threaten God's people.

262

'And who's gonna give us victory?' the soldier asked the crowd.

'Dagon!' the people roared. The soldier looked over at the priest, who nodded approvingly. This entertainment was proving to be more enjoyable than he'd supposed. No problem. He could be flexible with the day's schedule if it excited the people and honoured their gods.

'Who's gonna give us victory over the Hebrews?' the soldier shouted again. 'Who's gonna help us butcher those little maggots?'

'Dagon! Dagon! Dagon!' the people roared.

The soldier raised his hand to the crowd. It wasn't often a middle-aged soldier got the limelight—and this one was enjoying every second of it. 'And what's Dagon gonna do to the pussy god of the Hebrews?'

The crowd roared with incoherent shouting. Drunk on the moment, the soldier loosened his belt and pulled out his manhood equipment. 'I'll show yas what he'll do to him!' And, with that, he strutted over to Samson and began to piss on his legs. The crowds exploded in laughter.

Goliath stood amazed—and disgusted. He knew they were going to mock Samson. But urinating on him before Dagon's altar? He looked over at the priest—even he seemed shocked. Hysteria had ignited the crowds, and not even the priest dared to stop this show.

At first, Samson had accepted his fate with dignity. He knew his torment was the result of his choices. But now, it was no longer just about him—he knew he was standing proxy for Israel and Israel's God. They weren't just urinating on him; their actions here were a sign of what they intended to do to God's people—and the rage was burning strong. He stretched his arm and called for Goliath, who came and laid his hand on his shoulder. The soldier finished his business and turned back to bathe in the applause of the crowd. 'Take me to the pillars,' Samson said.

Goliath complied. Samson reached out his hands and felt the stone surfaces—his blood running down one. 'Catch your breath here,' Goliath said. 'I'll talk to the priest and insist he end this.'

'No!' Samson shouted back. 'I'm gonna end it.'

'You're half dead, Samson. You're not ending anything. Now you wait—'

'Goliath, you've been fair to me. But today, I'll make sure that the Philistines will do no more harm to my people. Get out of here, quick!'

Goliath couldn't hold back his unbelieving smirk. 'Good to see you got that fighting spirit back, but—'

'Why do you think I, a singular Hebrew was such a threat to

your leaders? How did I manage to kill so many? It wasn't my strength. Heaven gave me the power.'

Goliath looked at him, confused. 'Why are you telling me this?'

'It's back. If you have any trust in my words, get out of this building now!'

Goliath froze. There was no way he could abandon his post. It was already an act of mercy that the Lords had let him live. 'I can't abandon a prisoner,' he said, 'Who knows what the warden might do to me if these guys killed you and I was reported missing from duty.'

'It's not me you need to worry about,' Samson said. 'I can't guarantee your life if you stay. Go, now!'

Samson's words struck Goliath with all the authority of another world. His future dreams flashed before him—all he would do once his years of prison labour were over. He looked at Samson's mangled face. 'I'm not sure it matters what my life plans are if I'm dead,' Goliath said and ran.

Samson rubbed his hands along the surface of the two pillars and tried to focus. The image of Malachi's head lying on the prison floor flashed into his mind—a good and innocent man killed just to increase the cruelty of his torture. A fury of rage took him. 'Lord, remember me. Please, God, strengthen me just one more time. Help me, in this one moment, get revenge on

The Oliver Anderson Trilogy

these Philistines for my two eyes,' he prayed.

His fingers slid along the surface of the pillar. Memories of the time he slipped his fingers in between a lion's teeth back in the Sorek flashed through his mind. His hands found the perfect place.

And Samson began to push.

44

WHILE EVERYONE CHEERED, laughed, and declared the praises of Dagon, Delilah stared at the circus in front of her. 'What's Samson doing here?'

'It seems the organisers thought it good fun to parade our most excellent Hebrew captive about,' Achish said with a grin.

'Did you know about this?'

'I might've gotten wind of it. Why? You don't mind, do you?'

'No, of course not.'

'He's only here thanks to you.'

'Yes, I suppose. But he's blind,' Delilah said. 'What happened to his eyes?'

'We felt it best to remove those. He won't be needing them for the work we have him doing now.'

Delilah relaxed her shoulders. 'Hm, I can only imagine,' she

The Oliver Anderson Trilogy

said and wrapped her arm around Achish's as she watched the torment of her old victim. Although it was unexpected, she didn't find his humiliation unpleasant—until her brother ran into the arena.

'Goliath!' she shouted, only to be drowned out by 3,000 others. She turned to her husband. 'And my brother? Did you do this?'

'No,' Achish replied sincerely. 'I suppose the warden assigned him to bring him over here.'

'I don't want him getting hurt—either by Samson or one of those soldiers. Do they work for you?'

Achish laid his hand on his wife's shoulder. 'I'm a general. All the soldiers work for me in one way or another. Don't worry. The soldiers won't hurt your brother.'

Delilah turned her gaze back towards Goliath and Samson. Seeing those two men together—having a conversation in front of this animated and frenzied mob—made her mind spin. She squeezed her husband's arm even tighter and watched as, without warning, her brother turned away from Samson and ran full speed out of the temple.

'What's Goliath doing?' she asked. 'Is he alright?'

'I don't know,' Achish said. 'Maybe he's getting something for the prisoner.'

'I should see if he's OK.'

268

Achish laughed. 'Typical. Always the big sister. You'll only embarrass yourself. Probably get in his way.'

'He might've gotten hurt. Come, let's go see him. He's your brother-in-law.'

'I'm not going anywhere. But leave if you must,' Achish said and sat back down.

Delilah looked to the side of the building where her brother had exited. She looked back at Achish and then at the exit. For a split second, Delilah imagined running away from this mob and grabbing her brother's hand and making off for their childhood home in Sorek. 'But...' she didn't finish. The thought of separating from Achish—and the risk of losing him—was too much. She sat next to him and squeezed his hand.

She turned to her husband. 'You're right. I think—'

No sooner had she began to speak to her husband than his head exploded. Brain and bone blasted into her face knocking her off her seat and onto the floor. She wiped her eyes and stared up at where her husband's body had been a second ago, only to see a large brick. That's when she heard tremors—as if the earth itself was quaking.

The cheers of the people turned to screams. Delilah managed to get on her knees and saw bricks falling from the ceiling. That's when the stampede began. Aristocrats began tripping over one another as they ran for the exits. Between the screams

The Oliver Anderson Trilogy

and the earthquake, the sound was deafening. She fought to breathe as the weight of the bodies piled on her.

Then everything went black.

45

THE ONLY NOISE they heard was the gentle hum of hospital machinery and the sound of William's heart monitor.

'Yeah... and?' Oliver asked.

'And, what?'

'Then what happened?'

'Happened? Well, Samson, along with 3,000 Philistines, died in the collapse of Dagon's temple—an act that saved Israel from invasion.'

'Samson died killing them?'

'Pretty much.'

'I'm not sure how I feel about that ending,' Oliver said.

'It's not the endin', not really. It's only the end of one chapter in the story of God's people. Ye see, soon, God'll bring the prophet Samuel and then King David onto the scene.'

Elise gave a silent laugh. 'Oliver, have you never heard about

Samson and Delilah before?'

'Well, no, I guess I haven't. It's not like my parents raised me on these stories.'

'As ye've probably heard, Elise, my son and his wife aren't believers.'

'Yes, I've heard,' Elise said.

'They don't follow the new and greater Samson.'

'The what?' Oliver asked.

'The more excellent Samson. The one Samson points to.'

'You mean—'

'Yes, I mean him—the Saviour.'

'The "Saviour"? What does the story of Samson have to do with Jesus?' Elise asked.

'That's one thing about my grandfather. He knows his Bible well and, to him, every story inside it, including all the ones I haven't read yet, whispers the name of the Saviour.'

'My parents told me about Samson and the other stories as a kid. But I don't see how Samson is anything like Jesus.'

'I didn't say Samson was like Jesus. I said he points us to Jesus.'

'Samson? But, how?'

'Think about it for a minute, sweetheart,' William said. 'Both men had an angel appear to their mothers before they were born, and then later to their fathers, telling them about the son

Samson & the Siren

they'd have. Both men are called rescuers. Samson saved the people of God from the Philistines. Jesus saved them from sin, death, and hell. Both men began their ministry at a wedding— Samson at his own and Jesus where he turned water into wine.

'Samson resisted Delilah's temptations three times and then failed, while Jesus resisted the Devil's temptations three times the wilderness and then went on to victory. Both were Jewish men condemned by foreign forces: Jesus by the Romans and Samson by the Philistines. And, most of all, both men defeated the enemy and rescued God's people ultimately through how they died.'

'Wow. I never thought it that way,' Elise said.

'So, maybe Samson's death wasn't as tragic as it sounded?'

'It was years before the Philistines were able to recover from that temple collapse and, by that time, God had raised up other leaders to protect Israel.'

'You'll have to tell me about them another time,' Oliver said.

'Ye have a Bible, lad,' William said. 'I need ye both to learn the stories so that ye can teach 'em to a new generation.'

'Us?' Oliver asked.

'Yes. I'm gettin' old, lad. I won't be around forever to tell these stories. Others need to pick up where I've left off. We have a whole generation of young people who know nothin' of the Scriptures at best—and who assume they're borin' at worst. We

The Oliver Anderson Trilogy

need holy storytellers that'll tell the ways of redemption to a new generation.'

'That's us, Oliver.' Elise said.

'What do you mean?'

'We might not tell them in the same way your grandfather does, but we've spent three years in a film and theatre school. If we haven't learned how to tell a story by now, we've sure wasted a lot of time.'

Oliver smiled. 'I guess you're right. Samson and Delilah *would* make a great film.'

'Just so long as ye don't have all the characters as vegetables,' William said with a wink.

'Huh?'

Elise laughed. 'Perhaps there's one good thing about missing out on a Christian childhood—you escaped those cheesy Sunday school cartoons.'

'Vegetables? Really?'

'Ye don't wanna know, lad.'

'Gotcha,' Oliver said. William yawned. 'Well, grandpa, I know you're younger than your age, but you look like you could use some sleep. Plus, Elise and I haven't eaten. We'll go out for dinner and come back in the morning.'

'Plus, I need to write that email to Ms O'Donnell.'

'OK, you two. Let me know about it in the mornin'.'

Samson & the Siren

'Of course, grandpa,' Elise said as she leaned in and kissed him on the cheek.

'Well, I'll sleep better with that,' William said with a grin. 'Oh, grandson.'

'Yes?'

'Bring me some of that, ye know, in the morning,' William said, his hand making a swig towards his mouth.

Oliver laughed. 'Whisky into a hospital? I don't know, grandpa. I'll have to see what my conscience says about that one.'

William gave a silent laugh. 'I suppose I deserve that. Have a good evenin' ye two.'

'Bye, grandpa,' they said and left the room.

EPILOGUE

WILLIAM SPENT HIS evening poking at the food the nurse had brought him for dinner and praying for Elise and Oliver. He prayed that they would find peace and strength to handle their battles in a way that honoured Heaven. Then, he laid his head on the pillow and dreamed of a Kingdom where there would be no more need for dissent—one with only a good and wise King.

As he slept, a chariot descended into the room. The good King had come to awaken the spirit of William Anderson and take him to his forever home. All the stories he'd ever told had hinted at this place. It was the one place William had always been homesick for, even though he'd never been. Now, for William, the ultimate story was just beginning.

The following day, Oliver returned to the hospital to find the news of his grandfather's death. He contacted his parents who

Samson & the Siren

came up North, and together they arranged a funeral fitting for a man like William.

Oliver found comfort in Elise's arms and promises of eternal life. For her part, Elise was always glad she had met William before he died. By spending a day with him, she would understand Oliver and many of his future decisions better.

The call to be storyteller may have skipped a generation in the Anderson family, but Oliver picked up where the Scottish preacher left off. The mantle the old man left in his solitary hospital room fell on Oliver's shoulders and, with the help of Elise and the talents he'd honed at film school, he began to tell Heaven's stories to a new generation.

Thank you for reading. Now what?

Indie-Authors like me depend on you. If you've enjoyed this book, please leave a review on Amazon and share it on social media.

Books by Joshua David Jones

The Girl and the Guardian is the first in the **Oliver Anderson Trilogy**. Meet Oliver and his Scottish grandfather as they explore the epic of Mordecai and Queen Esther in the beautiful but cruel city of Susa, Persia.

In *The Genesis Ghosts,* Oliver encounters the dark and violent tale of Judah and Tamar, where Judah faces a ghost from his past.

Elijah Men Eat Meat (non-fiction) is a book of short, punchy readings following the life of Elijah, Jezebel, and Ahab. Great as a devotional.

CPSIA information can be obtained
at www.ICGtesting.com
Printed in the USA
LVHW111054011121
701665LV00013BA/532/J